THUNDER LA BOOM

ALSO BY
ANNE STEINHARDT

The Healthy Season

thunder

la bo

A NOVEL BY

Anne Steinhardt

A RICHARD SEAVER BOOK

The Viking Press / New York

To my father

THUNDER LA BOOM

I'm standing here by the door at Obie's, remembering the first time I saw Callie enter this din of light and music, with that timid smile flashing on and off like the blue and orange neon above us:

OBIE'S
GLOBE-A-GO-GO CLUB
"Nude" Entertainment

Right over my head the largest of Obie's six amplifiers is wailing away as usual, but tonight I'm wearing ear plugs and what I get is more sensation than sound, like an underwater explosion. The sign flashes and all the Day-Glo signs around the door explode and subside along with it:

ONE DRINK MINIMUM

Show I.D.

No one under 21 admitted

This week
LINDA, HEATHER, CYNDI
"LIVE" from L.A.

With the same rhythm I handle the present and flash on the past, orange and blue, take dollars, tear tickets, and remember the night four or five months ago when I first saw Callie. I remember she was wearing something brave and shiny and black, the Daughter of Fu Manchu Meets San Jose. Behind her came the other two, Kathy and Libby Lou, all dressed up, looking even more scared, stupefied by that jungle BOOM BOOM BOOM—"Lak a sex-a machine"—the lights, and the smell that hangs for three feet around the building, a combination of beer, smoke, sweat, piss, perfume, disinfectant, rut, a general stale gaminess so dense it takes impressions, like clay.

There were the usual stragglers around the door, wondering if it was worth the dollar cover charge to get in, or decompressing on the way out.

Men walk out of Obie's with X-ray vision. All that naked flesh leaves residual images on the eyeballs; you look at an ordinary chick and see right through her clothes.

Cynosure of the X-ray eyes, bombarded by the

noise and the smell, the three chicks, in a terrified phalanx, none of them looking over twenty, marched into the red gloom. The stragglers made moist noises and craned after them. I did too, twisting on my stool and looking through the lattice wall that blocks the stage from the entrance.

I remember it was particularly frantic at Obie's that night, probably a Friday or Saturday, when I'm running girls to the manager all night for change from the pay-day twenty-dollar bills and the used-car salesmen in iridescent suits stand six deep around the door, elbowing each other and yukking while I make the change and yell in the ten-second pause between songs for the owner of the blue Mustang to please come out and unblock the green Chevy, and everyone is getting drunk, even at seventy-five cents a beer.

The girls had gotten a few feet past the door into this crowd before freezing at the sight of Fat Mary, flat on her back on the spot-lit stage with her legs spread toward the audience.

Up front, an old Chicano in a straw hat yelled a few words of ecstatic Spanish and fell out of his chair. His beer went sideways, dousing a neighboring hard-on. There was a scuffle.

Slate, Obie's six-foot-eight spade bouncer, brushed past the girls.

The old guy's *amigos* hauled him back up. There were shouts and clapping. The old man signaled his ascendency with the classic, and at this point totally redundant, roar: "TAKE EET OFF!"

Two bar girls closed in their G-strings and neon make-up to hustle beer on the petrified chickies, who were clutching each other, twisted like a Laocoön with a half a dozen groping arms for the snake, as Fat Mary casually pumped, in front of eighty dripping eyeballs, her widespread cunt.

"Your love just like a Yo-Yo!" went the jukebox.

Mary saw me through the lattice. She patted her mouth in pantomime boredom, rolled her eyes, and yo-yoed on.

Some stragglers who had taken advantage of my distraction to peek in decided in a hurry to pay their money. I went back to my tickets and forgot about the girls. I gave them three minutes before they decided being file clerks wasn't so bad after all.

I'd been doorman at Obie's for only a few weeks back then, and God knows I'd never done anything like it before, but already I'd seen enough girls come in to tell the amateurs from the experienced dancers. Just coming in a group meant something—the pros tended to show up alone. They also didn't waste time dressing up for auditions; they knew managers don't give a flying suck what a girl looks like with clothes on, plus it being better not to stand out— any more than a lone chick in a crowd like this can help, anyhow—because only a hooker actually wants to attract that collective X-ray eye.

Actually, except for these groups of new girls that wandered in a few times a week, being doorman at a bottomless joint was pretty humdrum, something I would never have believed a few weeks ago myself. Take any man's vision of paradise, and whatever else is in there—Coupe De Villes, Stradivari—there's sure to be an endless supply of uninhibited dancing girls. But after a week of ass and cunt twinkling at me from all angles eight hours at a go, I was bringing things to read when I got bored.

The most stimulating part of my new occupation was the Buzzer.

The Buzzer was an ordinary doorbell across from me on the wall. It attached to an alarm at the bottom of the stage. I was supposed to hit the Buzzer at the least sign of cops, even a car cruising by out front. The alarm was loud enough to penetrate the music and general mayhem and send the dancer flying naked through the crowd to the ladies' room. Meanwhile, another dancer with her costume on runs up on stage and when the cops march through the door with these we-know-and-you-know-that-we-know-and-we-know-that-you-know-that-we-know shit-eating smiles, they find this other dancer with whatever change she was making at the time she was diverted sticking out the top of her bra, wiggling demurely in her legal quarter inch of sequins.

All this in honor of the fact that topless-bottomless was illegal in San Jose, and we could all get arrested— managers, bouncer, goons, and doormen—although the cops are really only interested in busting the girls. They never bother the customers, but the customers don't know this, there's nothing clears out the bar faster than the sight of a cop, except maybe the night some maniac lobbed a teargas bomb into the middle of the crowd, or that other night when somebody set fire to the ladies' room.

The cops were aware of this effect, which was why they went through with the whole farce, just to hassle us out of customers. They certainly weren't there to arrest anybody, because when they really wanted to catch a girl with her pants down they sent in a plain-clothesman.

Just the same, when I spot the car I hit the Buzzer and BLATT BLATT BLATT! a noise like those wails they set off in atomic-evil-island movies after the good guys have turned the reactor up to broil. I always gave it three for good measure, and by the third blast all the guys in the bar wearing a suit and tie were jammed around the door, jacket collars turned up, eyes darting behind the hands over their faces; I could see them picturing their wives reading the headlines across the breakfast table:

SAN JOSE TOOL-AND-DIE EXECUTIVE NETTED IN BOTTOMLESS RAID

When they finally managed to push out the door, it always turned out that four or five of them were blocked in by some other car. Confusion and hysteria set in in the parking lot.

The Buzzer was bad for business, but it was also good for business. Everybody got an illicit rush. Prohibition must have been like this; a ratlike figure races down a dark alley, hits the 1929 version of the Buzzer, a wall slides, and when Elliott Ness arrives all he finds is five couples in evening clothes waltzing around a punchbowl of lemonade.

By the end of my first few weeks on the job I'd had plenty of dry runs on the Buzzer, but my first real raid didn't take place until the night I'm describing, with Callie and her friends wedged in by a wall of tumescence, staring in disbelief at the stage.

Slate was in back dissuading someone from using someone else's head for a cue ball, Whitey and Joe, the two managers, were in the office, and I was on my stool by the door when some dude in the front row jumps up and starts waving a badge.

After a while it go so I could spot plainclothes as easily as uniforms. It's the mentality. All around the spades are bopping and jiving and the Chicanos are falling out of their chairs and the car salesmen are timidly trying an obscene yell or two, and in walk these two big dudes, always in pairs just like Friday and Gannon, with that way of holding themselves too: Frankenstein learning to walk. They sit down on opposite sides of the bar, which is the dead giveaway because real car salesmen hang together for immoral support; they order one beer for which they leave no tip, and they immediately record the expense in a small book.

Sometimes they send in a rookie just for the experience. Whenever you see someone in a pale blue Dacron windbreaker, brown slacks with pleats, a baseball hat with obscure insignia, and tennies, and the dude's shining a flashlight on a girl who is already illuminated by five hundred watts of spotlight, that's a rookie cop.

At the time, though, the first thing I knew was Whitey and the manager and this dude were walking out the door, and Whitey said, "Pete, this is a bust —take over. Put Slate on the door, and start calling girls. Get those three new chicks up there right away. See you in a couple of hours."

He was smiling, and the plainclothes cop was smiling and Joe was smiling. It was all so relaxed I remember thinking he was putting me on. But then the patrol car pulled up and the suit-and-tie boys started bottle-necking at the door, trying to look like they all just happened to wander in to use the cigarette machine.

The girls came out of the dressing room in street clothes. Fat Mary pressed a bottle of pills in my hand as she passed. Lynn was crying. Miss Rochquel Heart swept by in the long fur-trimmed coat, leading with her nostrils. Sandy gave me her old man's number on a matchbook cover.

Cars were pulling out of the lot every which way —thunks, tinkle of smashed taillights, honks—the confusion sorting itself out in the wake of the patrol car, which cruised off like the leader in the parade.

I tried to pin down a strange feeling. It was the silence, I realized. There were no girls left to punch the music.

And here I was, in charge of this weirdly quiet bar, with no dancers and no customers except for one old dude asleep in his chair and the usual gang of elegant spades around the pool table. Did they even know we'd been raided? Miles of spot-lit flesh quivered; underneath overcoats and hats and hands other flesh loomed in empathy like sea anemones in tides of smoke until the sweating dancer, the sweating men, and the howling jukebox seemed a force fit to split the building right down the middle and sweep us all out to sea. And in the midst of this thunder a shark in a bottle-green stretch jump suit with a big white L over the left breast strokes with the precision of a heart surgeon the eight ball off two rails—Yo-Yo!—into the far pocket.

"Hey, man," yelled one of them now, "somebody punch some music. I can't shoot straight with all this quiet."

Slate was leaning over me, yelling in my ear, which is normally the only way to make yourself heard at Obie's. His breath was strong and sweeping as a lion.

"I got the girls here for you," he yelled. "They was *leaving*." This last with amusement, as if there were any chance of leaving this place so easily once you came.

He had his arms around the girls, two under his left arm, Callie under his right.

His right hand was squeezing, traveling, squeezing.

I got my first good look at her—big dark eyes, big mouth. Big. She was still as a mouse in a paw.

Slate yelled down at them.

"Seeing as there seems to be a shortage of customers, we all got time to play Construction. You girls ever play Construction before?"

"I beg your pardon?" Callie murmured.

"Construction! That's the game where you lay down on your back. And I climb on top. And *blacktop* you. Haw haw haw!"

At this point it looked as though Callie had gotten a sudden urge to tango. She bent at the knees and slid back against his arm.

Slate took this for a fit of appreciation.

"Hey, I got another one. Any of you girls know the difference between a French rabbit and an American rabbit? See, the American rabbit go hippity hop . . ."

It was the first time I ever saw anybody in a dead faint.

". . . and the French rabbit go lickety-split. Get it? haw haw! *Lickety*-split!"

If I were a chick I'd probably have fainted myself the first time I ran up against Slate. Or Obie's. San Jose. Any of it.

My first time wasn't at night. It was two in the afternoon; no flashing lights, no stragglers, even the music turned down a little, in deference to the housewives in the shopping center next door. It was still a kick in the stomach.

I'd been on the road with Whitey since six that morning. Whitey picked me up hitching outside L.A. I was heading north after a month in Mexico. I'd been waiting for an hour, shivering, watching the sky lighten. I was surprised when an immaculate white Corvair stopped. The driver was a boyish-looking dude in a red, white, and blue jacket, all flash and fringes. When I got in the car I saw it was suede.

There was a tape deck, the heater was on, and as soon as we were on our way the dude lit up a doobie and passed it over. He pointed to a bag on the back seat filled with fruit and pastry. The whole thing was unreal after the hour alone with the dawn and my last ride in the back of a pickup next to a V-8 engine.

Whitey told me his name, and I flashed on a pretty kid with white-blond curls out the sides of a sailor hat. His hair was darkened, but Whitey still had that kind of face—spoiled little mouth, delicate features. He looked around eighteen, and I was surprised when he told me he was twenty-two, a year younger than me.

I told him a little about Mexico and how I was on my way to rough it in Alaska with my brother. He said topless dancers make a fortune in Alaska.

Then he told me about helping his stepfather run this theater club. That's exactly what he called it; a theater club. I remember the picture these words conjured, a combination Old West saloon and opera house, player pianos, ushers, sawdust, balconies, with ladies in feathers and gowns slit to the hips. I was in a dinner jacket checking membership cards.

Because just like that, because we were the same age, or he liked my looks, or whatever, Whitey asked me if I'd like to come in for a while, a couple, three weeks, pick up some bucks for the rest of my trip just sitting on my ass collecting money at the door. He said he'd even put me up with his mother. I said far out.

Looking back, I can't decide why I accepted so quickly, or at all. I'd gone down to Mexico to look up my mother. Mother split San Francisco when I was nine years old and my brother Robert fifteen, took her Steinway baby grand and her Baldwin acrosonic and headed south—she'd always had a thing about the tropics, she'd sit shivering in our living room in Pneumonia Gulch and talk about palm trees, sun, frangipani.

My father took it philosophically. After some years, more or less in self-defense, he'd taken up an instrument. Mother said he had no talent and made him play his saxophone in the basement, next to the furnace. When she left he was able to practice upstairs.

Robert didn't seem to mind much either, but then Robert was always an independent soul, like when he was nine or so deciding he didn't want to finish practicing that day; when Mother insisted, he picked up his little half-sized cello and bashed it over a dining-room chair. I bet that's when Mother really started thinking about leaving.

Me, on the other hand, although I hated the violin just as much, I kept on practicing even after Mother left. Especially after Mother left, because it must have been in the back of my head that if I practiced like a good boy she'd send for me. I wrote her propaganda letters: "Dear Mother, how are you, I am fine. Today I started Kreutzer. . . ."

There was talk of my coming to join her as soon as she was settled, which turned out to be a long process. I finally made it down there when I was twelve, not to stay, just for a visit, but I figured once I was there I could persuade her. I had my arguments worked out. I was a pretty self-reliant little chap, baching it the way we did; I could cook for her, I knew how to shop, I could even sew.

Mother had come to roost in Acapulco and was working nights in a piano bar in a hotel. I spent every night for two weeks in that smoke and gloom listening to my mother, who used to sit at the Steinway with tears running down her cheeks over Greig and Rachmaninoff, do "Perfidia" and "Tico Tico Toc" on a gold-painted piano with a tip glass on top.

It finally penetrated that despite having won my

first competition at age seven, despite all the arpeggios, Mother did not want me with her.

After that we wrote sporadically, but she was out of my life. Then a few months ago some heavy things happened and I decided it was time to try again, adult to adult. I wrote I was coming and hitched on down, but when I got to the last address I had Mother wasn't there. They said she'd left almost a year before. She wasn't working at the hotel any more. I ran down all the leads I got. Nothing. Mother had just upped and split, and she obviously didn't want to be followed.

The whole depressing thing was climaxed by my visa running out and a week in a Mexican jail. When I got out all I could think about was finding Robert. I hadn't seen Robert since he had started traveling. He'd been to India with a college professor looking for a guru; he'd shipped out to the Philippines and sent us boxes of cigars; now he was up in Alaska working the salmon boats. From what he wrote it seemed he'd been adopted by the Indians up there. I was thinking maybe they'd take me in too. I was willing to give up on a family being biological, but I sure was hurting for some kind of connection. So why did I sit in a white Corvair and tell a stranger I'd stay a while?

We pulled off 101 at one of the San Jose exits and drove past miles of used-car lots, shopping centers, trailers, and low concrete buildings with firm names ending in ONIC, COM, NIX. We passed a paper-products factory, a steelworks. Whitey turned off the main drag at a street with a big faded sign: SANTA CLARA COUNTY ANIMAL SHELTER. There was a garage, a trailer sales, the shopping center, and then Obie's.

A low concrete building in back of a parking lot with two cars in it. The first thing I flashed on was the painting on the sign over the door, a mottled swollen shape with something sticking out of it. A globe with a greenish pseudopod. Either something jerked the painter's arm while he was working on the outline, or he was a fan of Dali. It took me a minute to realize the droopy bulge represented a tit, a big planetary tit with the nipple swelling in the southern portion of the Chinese People's Republic.

Globe A-Go-Go.

We walked inside.

At two in the afternoon there are no bodies to break up the outlines, none of the demon energy that transforms and brings even this place its own peculiar fulfillment. The first time I walked into Obie's, all I saw was a longish barroom with a low ceiling. There were two stages facing each other across the bar. There were tables and chairs in the middle of the floor. Two guys were sitting at a long bar, looking at themselves in the mirror. The mirrors were all over the place, angled behind the stages, on the walls, reflecting each other; clear, smoked, and the cracked-looking kind shot with gold and black.

My nose and eyes were still adjusting when a beer mug materialized out of the gloom, backed by a near-naked girl with an expression like a barracuda.

"Mark it a spill!" yelled Whitey.

The girl rearranged her face, but the smile was for Whitey. Another one in baby dolls came over and clamped herself against him, lips to his ear. A girl in silver boots came out of a door and waved.

The pale kid in plastic hippy threads was suddenly looking impressive. It was partly the light, the red and orange bulbs that washed out any ambiguity along with the rest of your imperfections; and partly, as he bent to listen to the one girl, his arm around the bare shoulders of the other, because Whitey *was* a big man around here.

He walked off with the girl in the silver boots, waving vaguely in my direction. I took it I was on my own for a while. I stood there holding my beer, wondering what to do. The girl walked up on one of the stages. I went and sat down.

Looking back, this was the one time in my career at Obie's that I sat down and watched the show like any other customer. I ended up seeing a hell of a lot of dancing, of course, and a lot of times when things were slow I'd get someone to cover for me and sit at the bar to watch a few sets. But by then I knew the girls, and I knew the trip. That first time I was a pure tourist, nursing a warm beer and staring up at my first bottomless dancer.

The girl on the stage was light brown, rosy in the light. She leaned against the wall in a bra and panties and high-heeled sandals, staring at something that did not exist in this place.

She had a sloping back that skied off into a magnificent spade jut of tight rump. The bra was the stretchy kind, and it held her breasts high and rounded. But the way she was leaning against the wall—it was more than just tired, it was: I don't give a damn where I am or who you are. It was a turn-off.

The Rolling Stones started thumping on "Brown Sugar." The brown girl pushed herself off the wall and began to dance.

She barely moved—a leg to the side, a slight turn to the head, her arms hanging loose at her sides. But everything kept the rhythm from the weaving head to the side-stepping sandals. "BROWN SUGARH!"

wailed the Stones, and brown sugar flowed under cherry lights, the slight rhythmic motion right on.

Even she felt it. Still the minimum effort, but the fingers curled a little, just a hint of beckoning, and her hips came forward, just a little. Her eyes closed on that denying gaze. The blue light flashed on, turning her to indigo and slate.

Still, she was dancing for herself, not for me. I wanted to go up there and shake her until she looked me in the eyes. Then I wanted to throw her down and fuck her.

The red and white lights flashed on again. The end of the music seemed to catch her by surprise. She reached in front and opened the bra. She turned back against the wall, and supporting herself with one arm leaned down and pulled off her pants.

There was no grace or consciousness of being watched. She just pulled them off with one hand like a tired housewife leaning against the dresser while a husband snores across the room. A voice called from the back:

"SHOW US SOME MEAT THIS TIME, BABY!"

She didn't acknowledge that, either.

I turned around, and there was a guy around fifty in a yachting cap. He was leaning back in his chair, legs sprawled, a big happy grin on his grizzled face.

"Now we see some of that dark meat," he called to me in a comradely fashion.

I was embarrassed. I was embarrassed for her, for the old guy, for myself, for the whole sad scene. I felt like going up there and apologizing to her. I want you to understand, Miss, that just because he is a man and I am a man doesn't mean we're both slobs.

But of course I couldn't, because actually I'm as

big a slob as the next guy, just more quiet about it. My eyes were riveted to her body.

Lou Rawls started to sing in a voice that matched this lady's style; relaxed, smooth. But she wasn't having any. She went back into her robot number. It was still something to watch.

The way you had to look up at the stage foreshortened her. The thigh and hip bones were prominent. The muscles worked in her thighs, and the back lighting haloed the double bumps of her ass through her legs, and the biggest thing in my field of vision was the textured black bush with chocolate drops swaying far above.

Lou Rawls sang about a natural man, and this natural lady moved like a machine. She went back to the wall.

"LET'S SEE SOME OF THE PINK, BABY!" yelled the yachter.

The music started, and she came out again, danced tight-thighed, went back. This time she leaned against the wall to put the underwear back on, hoisting her boobs in matter-of-factly.

"I'm so tired I'm even tired of being tired," she said in a flat voice to nobody. She walked down the steps, and as she passed by I was surprised to see how slight she really was.

The barracuda trotted to the stage. Tiny, over-made-up eyes, badly bleached hair. But as the first one shrank when she left the stage, so this one grew as she climbed the steps. The lights rounded her; her hair was a back-lit nimbus, and here we have, gents, not a post-pubescent with skinny legs in Woolworth's undies for the whory housewife but a wild little bait, the kind every convertible needs to go down in a thunder of bourbon and potato chips, an adolescent fantasy sheathed to sleazy perfection in shiny elastic.

This one was the exact opposite of the last in energy. She burst into motion at the first note of her music. All her songs were fast. She waved her arms and ran around, every so often kicking one leg high and landing with a tiny leap. It was the one coordinated movement in her gallop. Somehow the little leap broke my heart.

She also related to the audience—that is, she kept a big smile on her face and looked right out at us. The half dozen or so other guys in the bar really got off on this one. She was their wild little thing, their kid sister, with the air of innocent exuberance to heighten the promise of depravity in that kick.

"Hey Sandy!" someone yelled. "When are you going to take dancing lessons?"

It was obviously a joke of long standing.

"When you stop being a dirty old man, Frank!" Sandy yelled back.

When the music started for the second dance, she pantomimed shyness about taking her top off—a "Who, *me*?" point of finger to chest, shrugs, grimaces, all the time racing around and flashing the high skinny leg. Finally she unhooked the bra, flung it aside, and strutted double time around the stage, hands over her head in the boxer's gesture, while the diminutive objects of this dumb show flapped frantically against her skinny chest.

In the fullness of time a sparse ruff was revealed, but to me the boobs were more interesting. They seemed to move independently, up-down-up-down, never missing a beat.

On her last dance she went all the way down after

a kick and I got a quick flash of very tight cunt. The ghost of a high-school desire for wild, sleazy little foxes, for frantic little bodies, swelled in me.

The inviting smile left her lips the instant her foot left the stage, though. As she walked past me, she gauged the level of my beer with an expert and evil glare.

Good old Sandy, the personality kid.

Four guys in work clothes walked in. The first girl was out from behind the bar before they'd gotten two steps inside the door. She stayed with them, remora and sharks, as they circled the room and ended up at a table next to me. One guy made a grab at the blue elastic jut, which swung smoothly out of reach.

"Can I get you a beer?"

"I'd rather have you, sweetheart."

"Yeah, bring us four. Do you dance, sugar?"

"Yes."

"Do you—you know—get it on?"

She walked away.

"Make them nice and cold!" yelled the guy, unwilling to be snubbed.

"Make it nice and *hot!*" said his friend, which broke them all up.

The empty stage waited, winking.

"NEXT!" yelled the yachter.

A hefty specimen strolled toward the stage. Her skin was brown, but her eyes were slanty, spade or Chicano-Chinese. There wasn't much the lights could do for this one. She had rolls of fat around her belly like a buddha, and tiny, drooping tits. She hauled herself up the stairs and leaned against the wall, weary but good-natured about it, not rejecting the whole scene like Lady Blue, not faking like

Sandy, just being what she was. Lou Rawls started telling it again, like, Don't you know what I mean, brother?

"REJECT!" bawled the dancer. A girl pressed a button behind the bar and Lou was cut off in mid-drawl.

"I just can't dance to that shit today," she said to no one in particular. Then she winked at me.

The wink said that there were days and days for all of us, now ain't there? The wink conveyed that I knew what she meant, just like Lou's voice conveyed that we all knew what *he* meant. It was beautiful. She'd included me in the scene, and for the first time I felt like maybe I wasn't an exploiter and a pig, but a guy entitled to some honest entertainment for an honest buck, just like a natural man.

I relaxed and swapped a wink with one of my neighbors.

"I'm so tired of being alone, I'm so tired of being alone, can't you help me, baby, it's so hard to be a man," wailed the jukebox.

I looked around the bar at the handful of lonely strays, and I flashed on what karma was working through Whitey to bring me here. Then I forgot it, turned back to the stage, and was treated to the unforgettable experience of Fat Mary.

Nobody had last names at Obie's. The girls were an endless stream of Lindas, Kathys, Pats, Tonis, Cyndis, Sandys, Dianes, and their Spanish counterparts, Theresas, Velmas, Marias, Annas. If two girls had the same name, one of them was given an epithet, like Fat Mary.

The managers were an endless stream of Joes, with the odd John. Except for an occasional exotic, like Miss Rochquel Heart, or my own discovery, Ms. Thunder La Boom, nobody used last names. It was always a shock to catch sight of a pay check and discover the dancer named Lollypop was actually somebody called Joanne Hackfeld.

Last names, I suppose, are too much a link with the normal world, families, responsibilities, the past, the future, things no one wanted—no one could bear—to think about inside these walls. First names are more flexible. Obie's brought out the secret desires of Marilyns to be Heather, Susans to be Lola and beyond—we had a Kitten, a Tiger Woman, a Mustang, a Grass Hopper.

Once when I first started working I met a girl

named Agency. She walked in the door and said, "Hi, I'm Agency. Where's the office?"

I fell right in love with her and her name, a silver name like Tiffany.

Then another dancer named Agency came in, and it turned out that's how girls who belonged to the local supplier of dancing girls talked about themselves: "Are you agency? Yeah, I was agency for a while. I'm not agency any more."

The two men who ran the agency I only knew as Prick-face and Fuck-face, epithets devised by my friend Paula.

It was months before I learned Whitey's name, more or less by accident from the card he had printed when he launched his own agency.

The card was pearlescent white, with GLOBE GIRLS: NUDE CUTIES printed in gold across the top, and then the famous globe with the nipple rubbing against the R in CLINTON ("WHITEY") PRINGLE, Talent Coordinator.

Clinton Pringle! Who the hell was that?

Even the boss was just Obie. I never heard anyone call him mister. Sometimes my checks came signed in a curious hand—European, or senile, or illiterate, maybe all three—with the name Obadiah Jackson, Jr. But it took me a long time to make the connection.

Whitey introduced his mother to me as Paula, which is what he always called her himself. When I look back on how I ended up at Obie's, I wonder if Whitey's offer to put me up had something to do with it. When he said I could stay with his mother I remember picturing a house with curtains, sunshine through the windows, a lady stirring something on the stove—the whole number. In my mind we were heading for that house when we pulled out of Obie's that first day, my eyes hurting from the sunlight, my ears still ringing and booming.

We drove past more trailers and burger pits and offices, then left into housing tracts and fields, over railroad tracks. Whitey pulled up at a motel that said Palm Oak Court. There was no sign of either tree, only some plastic tulips in a bed of red clinkers. The rest was asphalt, with low green stucco units in a U around it.

Out of the cubicle marked OFFICE stepped a woman in bright pink hot pants with the same-color scarf over blond hair. She had number-one legs. Not until she got close did the quality of her skin let on her age.

Her light eyes, set in deep circles, looked me over, then passed to Whitey.

"What the hell took you so long, prick-face? All hell's been breaking loose around here. That fucking plumber came again and left three inches of shit on the floor in number twelve. . . ."

Paula talked very fast, with a lisp—face came out "faith," loose came out "looth." She rambled on about plungers and ball cocks, and Whitey just smiled, letting it all wash over him, while I, fresh from Fat Mary, struggled to stop stripping her right down to the follicles.

I was having my first experience with the X-ray eyes.

A cunt. Man, a cunt is something else.

I don't mean that fuzzy isoceles they show even in *Playboy* these days. I'd seen plenty of that during my Grass Valley summer with the freaks, but there's a big difference between other guys' old ladies prancing around in postures of yoghurty liberation and the things Fat Mary did. I guess the closest to Fat Mary

I'd ever come was shining a flashlight on Deborah Turner when we were both ten playing a game I'd invented called Archeology; my father's blankets were a tomb, and I was the explorer, and she was an Egyptian mummy—

More recently there were snootfuls of Mrs. Matteo, my violin teacher's wife, but I was under the covers without a flashlight this time. My half a dozen or so other chicks I just rammed it in, not wondering about topology, just thankful I'd managed to find the hole. The one chick I lived with was very shy.

What Fat Mary revealed to me was cunt in its existential purity. The flaps! The palps! The crenelations and bulbs and creamers and sugar sacks! The goanies! The goanies!

There was a guy who'd come in, sitting on the other side of me, who said in a brisk voice, "You see that? That kind of line? That's an episiotomy scar."

"A what?"

"Episiotomy. I used to be a male aid. See these things all the time. Doctor cuts to let the baby's head out. It heals in a regular line like that. Otherwise it tears and you end up with your regular scar tissue. Get it?"

"Eh."

"See?" Right—*there*." He was half in my lap with clinical zeal. I nodded just to get him out of my way. Actually I wasn't sure. There were so many goodies down there, and the whole thing was moving—the flaps! sliding around over itself—good god, she was controlling that, it just squeezed in time to the music!

"ONE MORE TIME!" several voices hollered.

"ENCORE!" I yelled, wiped out.

Now, half an hour later, I was looking at somebody's mother to whom I had just been introduced, and it was like there was an anatomical diagram pinned to her midsection. I tore my eyes away, but there wasn't much distraction offered—on one side of the motel a gas station, on the other a coffee house with a CLOSED sign in the window.

"Forget about the bathrooms, Paula," said Whitey. "I want you to think where you're putting Pete."

"I'm sorry, Whitey, I'm not even talking about it. I told you last time, with that guy who ran his car into the office, I'm not running an asylum for your friends. Tell me, what alley did you drag this one out of?"

She smiled to show there was nothing personal, just a general reaction to people who looked like they had last slept next to a V-8 engine. But I was hep already. I sensed there was no real anger in Paula, just a kind of energy-releasing static. I did what Whitey was doing, just let it flow over. I watched her while she talked. There were the circles under the eyes and the mellowed-out skin, but her figure was good and her legs perfect. I couldn't equate her with a son Whitey's age; she looked thirty-five, forty at the most. Also, mothers don't look at you the way Paula did, as if there was a diagram pinned to *me*.

"'O.K., Petey, for you I'll kick somebody out," she finally said. I appreciated the emphasis. She was including me in a friendly league against Whitey, the ingrate, who never thought of the trouble he caused her. My mother used to play the same game, in a heavier way, aligning me with her against Robert, the bad one.

I remember wondering if there were also other meanings in the "you," but at the time I was too tired to play, beginning to give out after eighteen hours on the road. I let myself be led to one of the cubicles

I came on the scene when Obie's was just getting back into operation as San Jose's gamiest location for "nude" entertainment. Obie's opened for the first time soon after the demise of the legendary Orr House, first of the bottomless joints in the area, where the girls got eight dollars an hour and seventy-five in tips in a single night, where it was always packed to the rafters and the customers stuffed twenty-dollar bills in the crack of a girl's ass. Further up the money could not go, because the girls had to wear strips of tape over their slits in accordance with some bizarre health law, since abandoned.

Obie took over an ordinary neighborhood redneck bar, built stages, raised the beer fifty cents, and opened topless. After a month they went bottomless, got busted, went back to topless, got busted, curtained off the stages and went straight, went broke, tried a week bottomless, got busted bad. Now, having collected enough from his myriad other sleazy enterprises, like the motel his ex-wife Paula ran, and beer joints from Monterey to Burlingame,

Obie was reopening with a new name, to bursts of publicity in all the coast papers—

TOPLESS! BOTTOMLESS! IT'S BACK AGAIN!

—the Buzzer, and to deal with the hassles, "a battery of legal talent," Obie's phrase, meaning one lawyer and a bail bondsman.

He also made plans to inject some class into the ranks of students and minority scuzzies bumping away under the winking lights. Hence Whitey's trip south to arrange getting girls from an L.A. agency; hence Peter Stern, and, soon after, Miss Rochquel Heart.

My introduction to Miss R.H., or the "speciality," as she was known, was through a photograph with the message underneath: "COMING" SOON: GLOBE A-GO-GO PRESENTS "LIVE" FROM BROADWAY "MISS" ROCHQUEL HEART.

I found this pinned in front of the door where no one who came in could miss.

"That's the specialty we ordered from L.A.," said Whitey, as if she were a pizza with the works.

The girl in the publicity shot was wearing a top hat, and there was a big fake heart-shaped mole on her cheek. After half a night of staring at the air-brush smile, I found myself pondering Obie's literary style. His use of quotes. "Coming" soon, indeed!—And that "Miss"—did the quotes there mean the title was only one of courtesy, this broad not only being four times Mrs. but, possibly, Mr. Schleckly, a forty-five-year-old transvestite?

I had a lot of fun with "live," but by 1:00 a.m. was prepared to admit that the ten possible interpretations I'd discovered couldn't have been intended, and the whole thing was just Obie's illiterate addiction to quotation marks, which were obviously meant, like "Miss" Heart herself, to add class to his act.

A week later the specialty arrived. An old white Triumph bumped into the Palm Oak, and out got a little figure in a scarf, wraparound shades, and a coat down to her ankles. The coat was trimmed with fur that looked just like the little dog dancing around her feet.

She shut herself up two doors down, in Number Eleven, and started sending out for things. I saw Slate, who lived in seventeen, drive off in the Coupe De Ville and come back with a big bag. Paula stopped by my room.

"Don't ask me what's going on around here. Some hooker who once washed glasses at El Cid is suddenly a big Broadway star. 'Would you mind so fucking *terribly* pressing these few little things for me? I must preserve my strength.' I know what kind of sick that one is." Paula tipped an imaginary bottle. "Never mind, the first time I find dog poop on the carpet, she's out, specialty or no specialty. Anyhow, lovey, here's the keys to the Mustang. Run down to Thrifty and get some Listerine and a box of plugs. Madame would appreciate it *ever* so fucking much!"

When I delivered the drugs to Number Eleven, the door barely opened.

"Thank you," came a hoarse croak. She really did sound sick.

That night things were cooking at Obie's. To begin with, I saw my boss for the first time. Whitey had told me that if some guy who said he was the boss ever tried to get in free I should make him pay, because that was a test, like the D.A. with the special plates who goes around parking in front of hydrants to commend the cops with the guts to ticket him.

It happened just like that. Around seven-thirty up walked a group of older types, two women and a man, headed by a small guy in one of those phony hunting coats with the straps and flap pockets all over it. He started to walk right past and I pointed to the sign: ONE DOLLAR COVER.

"Don't give me that shit, fellow, I'm your boss!" he yelled.

"Boss or no boss," I yelled, "you'll have to talk to the manager."

"Good boy. What's your name?"

"Peter."

"Here you go, Peter. Keep the change."

He handed me a five for the four of them, tapped me on the cheek, and they walked in.

I guess Obie was around sixty. He looked like a playboy in some old magazine—pencil mustache, brilliantine hair. His face was lumpy, the eyes beady and intelligent. His partner was big, with jowls. The women looked like sisters, two little witches in crooked black skirts. One of them was wearing white socks that were slipping into the heels of her shoes.

They sat down at the end of the bar you can see from the door and proceeded to order round after round. The girls swarmed at that end of the bar, knocking each other aside with their hips and elbows like the roller derby. The boys hung around too: Whitey, Slate, the manager, and Gerry, a good-looking dude with a heavy Southern accent, just turned twenty-one—he went around for two days waving his driver's license in everybody's face. I wasn't sure what Gerry's function was, except he was there every night, and he packed a gun that he waved in people's faces a lot, too.

There was lots of laughing and ducking and backslapping.

". . . and the French rabbit go *lickety*-split!" I heard Slate explain during a break in the music.

"Yeah." Gerry was laughing, finishing some joke of his own." "But *Ah* fucked a *duck* foe a *buck!*"

Obie roared and ruffled Gerry's hair.

The crones in their ankle socks and crooked black skirts sat quietly in the corner, sipping cokes, watching the dancers with narrowed eyes.

Obie's was always crowded in those days, before the novelty wore off again. The crowd was classier, too, not just working stiffs and a few local white collars, but downtown dudes out slumming with their wives and girl friends.

Before the cops made us crack down we had hookers, too, and pimps out to recruit among the dancers; watching the crowd's reaction to her dance is a good way to judge a girl's appeal. Hookers in hot pants and boots and outrageous wigs cruised in and out with new tricks every twenty minutes. There was one set up in a VW camper right in the parking lot.

It was all so low that it came right out the other side of sleazy into a certain sordid splendor.

There were a lot of girls that night too: five dancers and two beer-sellers, which made the crowd happier than the usual three lone hacks wiping themselves out dancing, hustling, and washing glasses in an endless cycle for eight straight hours.

The five dancers, and the boss, and it being the night of the big specialty, worked some kind of hype on the bar. The girls were going up two at a time, one on each stage, and really working out, competing with each other. The beer-sellers forgot to hustle and danced down on the floor, ringed by customers. Men screamed and howled and banged their glasses on the tables. The demons were out.

On nights like these the balls go wild on the pool table and there are fists bunched in collars all over the bar, with Slate wading from group to group, after which it turns out that the two dudes were just having a friendly arm wrestle, thanks a lot anyhow.

Whitey got into a push-and-shove match with some dancer's old man. Suddenly, nobody at that end was watching the girls any more, they're all learning to see Whitey and this dude thrashing on the floor at Obie's feet. The two crones watched, sipping their cokes. "Hey, Pretty Mama, let your Daddy in," go the six amplifiers. A dancer is taking off her pants.

Since it was a crowded night, the dancers were alternating stages, and in between sets the crowd moved in great peristaltic surges from one end of the bar to the other, to lap against one or the other stage. The beer-sellers surged along with them, because mugs tended to get forgotten or lost or spilled in the migration, and in the trough between dancers you could hear their high voices: "Would you care for another beer, sir? Can I get you another? You want some more?"

There was a longer than usual break in the music. I saw a small figure, wrapped like a mummy, come out of the dressing room. The jukebox started in on "D.O.A.," a macabre ballad in which a smack freak croaking from an overdose in a police ambulance describes his sensations to a background of sirens.

A hand in an elbow-length black glove appeared

from behind the stairwell partition and waved provocatively.

"AH SEE THEY FINALLY GOT SOMEONE AROUND THIS PLACE WHO KNOWS WHAT SHE'S DOING!" Gerry yelled.

On the wings of this accolade the entire figure presented itself. There she was. Miss Rochquel Heart.

There was a profusion of rhinestones—her neck was one big choker, rings on every finger, a rhinestone butterfly in an obviously fake mane that cascaded right down to her ass. The way it all winked and twinkled under the lights was psychedelic.

It was hard to tell about her figure. She was covered from head to toe, and her painted face stuck out of the rhinestones like a puppet head, nothing moving but the nostrils.

She poised for a moment, all twinkles and nostrils. Then she began to dance.

Well, not really a dance. All she did was walk around the stage, stopping every few steps to strike a pose. At intervals a veil landed on the carpet. She tossed the Dynel tresses a lot.

As the addict gave a final spasm to the dying wail of the police ambulance, the final veil came off. There she stood in a pile of nylon, wearing stockings and a garter belt and long black gloves. Her boobs were miniscule, and drooped. I had to give it to her, she wore them like diamonds.

Another song, and off she marched again, stalk, pose, flare, toss, stalk, pose, flare, toss. At one point she turned her back and touched the floor with one hand while the other came between her legs, the black fingers spread over the cleft. She could also contract each of her buttocks separately.

The guys whistled, but they were getting impatient. Many requests in the classic mode:

"TAKE IT OFF! GET DOWN TO BUSINESS, BABY!"

Another whole song peeling off stockings with much stroking of legs by a large purple feather.

The guys were whistling and stamping. They wanted meat.

Finally the big moment came. The three-hundred-dollar-a-week fancy L.A. agency twat was about to be revealed. She unhooked the garter belt and flung it aside, standing there in the long black gloves and—good Christ!

Her pubic hair was shaved in the form of a valentine, with a rhinestone arrow twinkling through the hairs.

Miss Rochquel *Heart*. Yeah.

Normally the atmosphere at Obie's is the emotional equivalent of that black sludge, a mixture of beer slops, ashes, and dirt that oozes out of the carpet and rots the girls' shoes so fast they need a new pair every few weeks. Dark, corrosive, homogeneous nights, of which only a few stand out in my mind. The night Callie came. The fire. The tear-gas bomb. The debut of Miss R.H. And the night she got punched in the eye.

The men didn't get off on Miss R.H. She looked good enough up there, she was a professional, but the trained buttocks behind and the sheared beaver up front didn't seem like real cunt and ass. The guys frankly preferred the skinny little girls in J. C. Penney's underwear who stumbled up the stairs still holding three dirty mugs and a quarter tip. They even preferred someone like Delise, my chocolate lady. Indifferent, disgusted as she was, Delise wasn't promising anything more than she had. She was real, a working girl doing a job, and they were working men, mostly, and they could dig it.

Well, when you're hot you're hot, and when you're

not, you're not, as Jerry Reed told us six dozen times a night. But Miss R.H. even managed to antagonize the girls. Between sets she sat in the dressing room retouching her make-up, changing costumes, and writing letters on lavender paper. When one of the girls staggered in all sweaty and disheveled to rest a minute, so they told me, she acted put out, as if they were disturbing her privacy. This dressing room wasn't even really a room, just some kind of long closet, like a storage space, which is what they also used it for: packages of bar towels, cartons of toilet paper, a ladder, empty beer kegs. There was a plunger in one corner, an industrial mop and bucket stewed gently in another. On one side of the dressing room was the men's room, which you could smell through the wall; on the other side, the cold locker for the beer, from which there was a constant seepage. You walked in the dressing room into a small Sargasso sea of beer, with bar towels floating on top, a few purple feathers, a cockroach drowning happy. There were notices all over the walls, hung by a succession of Joes: GIRLS WILL BE FINED FOR . . . ANYONE CAUGHT CATCHING SPILLS WILL BE . . . ALL CLOTHES NOT ON HANGERS WILL BE . . . NEVER FOR ANY REASON . . . DO NOT . . .

Successions of managers, fed up with the girls' complaints about the smell, had tried every deodorant known to man, and they were all at work in there now simultaneously. Three toilet-bowl fresheners hung on the clothes bar, there was an ecological chaos of air sprays—Desert Bloom, Mountain Glade, Spring Meadow, Autumn Spice—a bottle of Airwick on top of the ladder, and, on the wall, the latest and most advanced attempt, a metal box that automatically released a mist of deodorant at preset intervals with a sudden whoosh it was easy to mistake for the lecherous hiss of a customer sneaking a look through the door.

No prize retreat, in other words, but here Miss R.H. made her stand; every once in a while she'd stick her head out the door, tap a girl charging by with two beers in one hand, four dirty mugs in the other, and a dollar between her teeth, and ask, in that aristocratic croak, if she could please have a glass of water.

Even so, nothing probably would have happened if the demons hadn't been out that night. The demons live in the jukebox on a diet of carpet sludge and frustration. A few times a month they break loose. When they're happy it's party time for a while, like the night of Miss R.H.'s debut. When they're not, watch out.

To start things off wrong, that night we had Angels in the bar. Every so often, half a dozen Angels pulled in on their choppers, raising so much dust and noise they even drowned out the music. They never gave any trouble, just played pool and sprawled around presenting a great deal of hairy, leathery surface, but they tended to make everyone nervous.

The guys in the iridescent suits got nervous on general principles; the manager got nervous because of the havoc the Angels could cause if they felt like it; the girls got nervous because when an Angel pinched one or grabbed her onto his hairy knee —anything short of raping her on top of the bar, and that too, come to think of it—there was nothing she could do. All the girls knew the grisly fate of the dancer who'd had a few words, not even with an Angel, but with a fellow dancer who turned out to be a biker chick.

There was one more thing. One of the Angels, a huge guy called Porky, was the only dude in San Jose large enough to take on Slate. Sooner or later this was going to happen, and when it did it was also inevitable that one of them would end up like the song, with ambulance sirens wailing Obie's out of business for a long time.

Nervously checking his gun behind the bar, Gerry dropped it at the feet of a nervous dancer who screamed and spilled her beer on it. Gerry lit into her. The girl got hysterical. The manager, trying to calm things down, told the girl she could take the rest of the night off if she wanted.

This is how he explained the thing to me later, anyhow.

All I knew was there was a sudden break in the music—someone had hit the reject button—and a hysterical voice yelling, "He's firing me because I'm menstruating! He's getting rid of me because I'm on the rag! He hates us! He hates women. The dirty rotten little . . . !"

I turned and saw this white freak the agency had sent over racing up and down behind the bar yelling in the faces of the startled customers. Gerry was standing there waving his dripping pistol.

"Shut up!" yelled the manager.

"No!"

"Shut up!"

"No!"

"Somebody shut both of them up, for Christ's sake!" yelled a dude.

The music started again. "Lovin' is what livin's all about," crooned the jukebox.

Slate put his hand over the girl's face and pushed her into the dressing room, but it was too late. Within a few minutes the bar was almost empty. Menstruation, hysterics, accusations—these were things that belonged to the outside world, along with marriage and wives. That's what they came here to get away from, for chrissakes.

We'd been raided by reality.

Things were dead for an hour or so; then the bar started filling up. The manager was daring to hope again when there was a sudden racket from the back, banging and screams so loud I even heard them up front.

Gerry and Slate raced toward the back. They came out of the ladies' room dragging a fat guy with his shirt hiked up. Slate had both his arms twisted high behind his back, and Gerry had the gun in his ribs. The guy was howling.

Demons!

This fat slob, this gray-haired loser, drunk on warm beer and cunt, blond cunt, dark cunt, tight cunt, cunt open, cunt, cunt, cunt nonstop, as many straight hours of cunt as a guy could take starting at twelve noon until two in the morning, this poor slob had gone berserk and tried to rape a bottomless dancer in the ladies' room!

The manager came out with his arm around the girl, a cute little girl who went to San Jose State and brought her books to work. She had her hands over her face.

We had to get the girl dressed and into a cab, still shaking and sobbing, keep the Angels from cutting the guy to pieces, and call the cops. And all this time Marvin Gaye kept singing about living and loving and the girls kept dancing and most of the customers never noticed a thing.

The cops hung around for a good hour. After it was

obvious the girls weren't stripping for the duration, most of the customers left for the second time that night.

Around eleven-thirty, just as the bar was beginning to recoup, our regular patrol car pulled in, and I had to hit the Buzzer.

Toni, a heavy red freak, was dancing. Upset by the rape, and never too well coordinated anyhow, she missed the bottom step and landed with her ankle under her. Slate lifted her up and raced for the dressing room, disappearing inside just as the first cop stepped inside the bar, like King Kong turning a corner one step ahead of the vigilantes.

Now we were two dancers short, but Miss R.H. refused to dance more than one set an hour—she'd be glad to show the manager her contract.

The manager was a game little Joe—he marched around his empty bar clapping and whistling over a half-dead dancer who'd been up there forty-five minutes—but I think what finally got him down was this chick, during her minute break, letting out a scream from the dressing room. She'd been in there straightening her costume, when suddenly something broke through the wall right in front of her eyes. Evidently some guy who got off peeping was standing in the men's room screwing maniacally away with a brace and bit.

By the time we got in there the bathroom was empty, but we found the hole and a pile of plaster on the floor.

It was only one o'clock, but the manager decided to pack it in. We got the few remaining customers out and locked the door. Normally the girls all pitched in to clean up, but Toni was sitting on the bar with her foot in the hot sink, Miss R.H. could not be expected to *wash ashtrays,* and that left Pat, a big muscular spade chick, wading through the debris revealed by the house lights, collecting glasses and ashtrays and muttering to herself, "Damn near dance you to death and pinch you to death and throw you in jail and now you can't even take a gooddam leak any more without they jump on you in the can."

I went into the office to do the door receipts. Suddenly we heard Pat's resonant drawl: "Oh yes you did, sister. You the only one here had the opportunity."

"You're wrong." Croak.

"You not calling *me* wrong. I know what I know."

"I don't care what you know."

"I know you don't care. You don't give jack shit for nothing around here. Well, you may be Miss Lah-De-Dah to yourself, but to me you nothing but a fucking ripoff. You give me back my money!"

"Pee-tah!" croaked Miss R.H.

I got out there just in time to see Pat land a good right to the side of Miss R.H.'s face.

"You tell her she better fork over with my bread," Pat yelled at me and stomped off to get dressed.

Miss R.H. just stood there with a hand to her cheek. I went back in the office and told Whitey I was taking her home. As we were leaving I heard Pat rounding off on Whitey: "I don't care *what* you say, mister . . ."

Miss R.H. handed me the keys. She still wasn't talking. The eye was swelling shut; I could see it outlined in the phosphorescent green of the arc lights.

"What are you doing for that cold?" I asked.

"I'm running around getting overheated and then I'm sitting in a freezing dressing room."

She made it sound like I was personally responsible. I shut up. But when we pulled up in front of Number Eleven she smiled and asked me in for a drink. Nothing heavy, said the smile. Just some company after a bad night.

I followed her in.

She turned on the lamp by the bed. In the little pool of light surrounded by shadows the room looked as cruddy and overinhaled as the one we'd just left. The bed was unmade, there were clothes and those filmy nylon tease things all over the place. The little dog that looked like a coat was pressed against the wall, wagging its tail and whining. There was a pile of little turds in the middle of the floor.

Miss R.H. got some toilet paper and lifted the mess off the floor. She came out of the bathroom holding a washcloth over her eye.

"That's all I needed," she croaked. "I got false hair, caps, a nose job—now I can get a glass eye."

She sat down on the bed and poured whisky into two Shell station bonus mugs. We clinked cups.

"I don't know what I expected," she said after a few swallows. "This place is strictly feeding time at the zoo. My agent must have been crazy."

She took a belt.

"I've had to be very careful about where I work. After Broadway, I mean. If I wasn't so restless I'd still be working up there. But I like to move around. Me and Faro, we've been a lot of places together. Here, Faro."

The little dog came over slowly. He still thought he might get it for crapping on the floor. She grabbed him by the collar, pulled his head between her knees, and tilted the glass in the side of his mouth. He coughed and shook his head.

"Don't waste it, dummy. Would you believe I had four of them when I had my apartment in the city, all identical? This one and Poker and Keeno and Blackjack. They all loved booze. They got so funny, lord, they used to crack me up. When I had to go somewhere, I paid the doorman to walk them. What do you expect when the poor thing's shut in for eight hours?"

Faro broke loose and retreated under the bed.

"You ever been to the Garden of Eden on Broadway?"

I shook my head. She looked at me the way Matteo did my first lesson when I told him I'd never heard of Viotti.

"You never saw a man without a jacket and tie. They had ads in the paper how they only want girls with college degrees. No joke. Jesus, my agent must have gone crazy."

She leaned toward me and held up the bottle. I shook my head.

"There's somebody waiting for me in L.A. who was very much opposed to me leaving the city. Very much opposed. But I'm here, right?"

She fluttered her nostrils. She'd been doing that trick so long she'd probably convinced herself it was a sign of real passion. But she didn't want sex. The look in that one eye gave her away. She just didn't want to be alone in a motel room in San Jose with a black eye and an alcoholic dog.

The whole thing was subtle enough to have missed, and that's how I played it. I yawned and thanked her and went back to my room.

I really was wiped out, but I couldn't get to sleep. I lay in bed looking out on the court. I saw Gerry pull up and go into his room. Paula came out of the office

53

and crossed the court. She knocked on Gerry's door. The door opened and closed.

I saw Miss R.H. come out of her room in the scarf and dark glasses and Faro on a leash. They walked off into the night.

The Coupe De Ville sailed in. Slate crossed over to the passenger's side and helped somebody out. It was Toni, the red freak. By this time of night she'd be so dopey she wouldn't know where the hell she was.

They went toward his room, Toni hobbling, Slate supporting her. She was about five-four, and very slender. Slate was a foot and a half taller and weighed at least three hundred pounds. I hoped Toni was good and out of it.

Toni was about to play Construction.

Just like that I decided to finish out the week, draw my pay, walk to the on ramp north and stick out my thumb. Relieved, I fell asleep.

"LAST CALL!" screams the manager.

With groans and thank gods, the girls rally like horses that smell the stable.

"Like one more for the road?"

"No thanks, honey. I'd like *you* for the road, though, heh heh."

"Heh heh yourself, you creep!" Because there's no more need to be nice, there's nothing more this guy can give, in a few minutes he'll be on his way home and eight hours of creeps and taps and gropes and quarters and grinds and sinks are coming to an end. Blessed two in the morning is here.

The jukebox goes off.

"That's it, folks. Drink up. We open again at twelve tomorrow."

The house lights are turned on, revealing the floor ankle-deep in butts, crumpled cigarette packages, gum, ticket stubs, the uncarpeted part puddled in beer, leaks from the sink, piss, and God knows what, with beer mugs lying on their sides, upturned ashtrays, pennies, peanuts, Kleenex, cubes of pool chalk, a pair of shades, broken glass, bottles, and hey, over there, a quarter, upon which three girls and the manager promptly jump, pushing and shoving.

The yellow house lights not only undo the mellow effects of the red, they perform the opposite alchemy. Everyone is suddenly ten years older, fifteen pounds fatter, wrinkled, gaunt, with stretch marks, appendix scars, and pimples that aren't even planning to come out for another two days.

The go-go dancers come out of the dressing room, tired women of various ages, some nineteen, some forty-five, in jeans and sweaters and glasses, carrying their costumes in paper bags.

Gerry and Slate herd the last customers out the door—with their usual impeccable timing the pool players have managed to start a new rack just at last call, insuring they can stay till the place is locked up.

The girls go into the office one by one with their banks, and face the last ordeal of the night. So many beers registered to their tap, so much money in the drawer, and if the numbers don't match, if the drawer comes up short, the girl has to make up the difference out of her pocket.

It's the end of Callie's third night at Obie's. I'm not counting the night they came to try out. As soon as she revived, the three of them got in their car and disappeared. I never expected to see them again.

But here was Callie, leaning over the sink washing glasses. Tendrils of hair were sticking out all over her head and her bra, not even a stretchy but a plain white, heavy-duty model, was slipping over her shoulders.

A customer on his way out leaned over the bar and took a good, deliberate look down the front of the bra.

Callie looked up and covered herself with soapy hands.

The dude leaned further over.

"C'mere, baby. I got to tell you something important."

Callie straightened up, wringing her hands.

"I beg your pardon?" she said.

This big girl had a surprisingly small voice, and she went around saying "I beg your pardon" every two minutes in this tiny, cultured voice and wringing her hands like a Russian tragedy. It was already a big joke around the bar.

"I said come *here,*" repeated the dude.

Callie leaned forward politely.

His hand shot out and grabbed her wrist. She was dragged halfway across the bar. Into her face he shouted, "I just wanted to tell you you got a beautiful clit. Haw haw haw!"

Callie's big eyes widened, as I'd been watching them do with great frequency for three nights now.

"I *beg* your pardon!" she said in that small voice. Her free hand twitched; I think it wanted to wring.

"I SAID YOU GOT ONE HELL OF A BEAUTI-FUL . . ."

"Closing time!" I yelled. "Let's go home, mister."

"You're not my type," the dude shot back, hanging onto Callie's hand.

Slate came over and said softly, "The bar is closed, brother."

The dude looked up, dropped Callie's hand like a dead clam, and scuttled for the door.

"And how are you feeling tonight?" Slate asked Callie.

"Surviving, I think. A bit tired, of course, thank you. And you?"

"FUCK YOUR FUCKING METER! I'M NOT

PAYING!" came an angry voice from the office.

"I beg your pardon," said Callie as Slate took her neck in his big hand. Once again her top half went slithering over the wet bar. Slate moved his fingers up to her cheeks and tested the swivel action of her head a few times.

"You got a old man waiting for you, mama?"

It was a question I'd been mildly interested to know myself. I was intrigued by this poor big dumb broad, with airs, yet, who'd been fucking up so righteously for three nights now.

Her two friends weren't hard to type. Kathy, the fresh-faced blonde, was a washout. About half of the newcomers fell into this category. For one reason or another they couldn't hack the scene, and they never lasted more than a week.

Kathy looked good, and the guys went for her, but she climbed the steps every time like there was a guillotine waiting at the top. The rest of the time she hid in the dressing room. After the second night she didn't come back.

Libby Lou was the opposite. Libby was a natural. Libby—short for Libra, she said, Lou for the hell of it—had one of those shapes that drain downward; breasts slender but full at the bottom with big, ground-seeking nipples, everything gravitating toward the ass, not one of those hard-packed spade ski jumps but nice and wobbly, no angle to it, just hanging off her like two fat marshmallows.

Libby's eyes were close-set, and her full face fell away toward the chin. She had a short, cupid mouth that exposed her front teeth; in profile she looked a little like a llama. Her skin was perfect, though, her long hair natural silver, and her eyes were big and brown. She was healthy and good-looking and when she danced, a steady, uninspired rhythm with one foot coming down hard on the beat, that gorgeous ass jiggled like a stone in a pond.

On the floor she waded right into the crowd, something that scared most chicks at the beginning. She hit a good pace right away, not wasting time picking her music, getting right back to selling after her set. She wasn't enjoying what she was doing —she never smiled—and she'd pass, in the course of the eversame nights, from distaste to accommodation to indifference, but Libby Lou had it together.

Callie, on the other hand—but who can categorize Callie? She was not, bravely, a washout; after the first disastrous night she came back for a second, and a third. Not, emphatically, a natural. To begin with, she was no beauty. I have to make an effort to keep that early Callie separate in my mind from what she became, but when she started dancing at Obie's, Callie was a cow. A big girl, almost as tall as I am, and at least thirty pounds heavier. The only thing that saved her was the long legs, although above the knees they tended to blend into the general puddle of a body whose next definition was an incongruously slender neck supporting a head too big for it.

The stage lights did their magic, and up there she looked like one of those big Maillot females you can dream of bouncing on top of like a little boy, lost in immensity. But why did she wear her hair like that? It was pulled back tight behind large, innocent ears and held down in back by legions of hairpins that littered the stage after she danced. In the course of the night more and more hair came loose in little curly corkscrews. By the end of the night it looked like she'd combed her hair with a cheese-grater.

And her costumes. Now she was wearing an old

bathing-suit bottom and a harness kind of bra. The first night she showed up in a pair of tights and a shawl. The manager made her borrow an extra costume from a girl who was five-two. All night long one boob or the other was popping out of the tiny top into some dude's face, and the elastic of the G-string cut a waistline around her hips. Pubic hair struck out around the little satin patch like cilia on an amoeba.

Her make-up was heavy even for Obie's, but up on stage it was O.K., staring eyes and big red-painted mouth like the *Perils of Pauline.* Unfortunately, by the end of her first set the make-up was all over her face; mascara ran down her breast like a line of ants and dripped sedately off her left nipple. God, did this girl sweat!

I'd never seen anything like it. It was hot up there under the lights, and the girls who worked out came down with a shine on their bodies, but Callie sweated like a longshoreman. She left slicks of sweat all over the stage. The next dancer said, "Sister, you worse than a mule. You better do something about that, I ain't about to break my neck on *your* mess."

"I beg your pardon," said Callie, wringing apologetically. The next time she went up she took the billiard talc with her and dusted the stage after she was through. After a languorous roll on the floor, her spade successor came up looking like a Hostess Ding Dong.

What Callie did on stage in addition to sweating a lot was also unusual. Her dancing had the effect of those very old movies that skip frames. The only thing she did in time with the music was wring her hands.

She spent time she should have been hustling beer doubled over the jukebox, nose pressed up to the glass. It was obvious that for all the names meant to her they might have been columns of Mongolian folk songs. She always ended up punching numbers off the cards the girls left stuck in the glass to remind them where their favorite songs were.

One time she ended up with a set of someone like Nina or Theresa, four heavy Latin rhythms headed by "Jungle Fever," in which some noisy chick has her eyeballs fucked out to a throbbing three-note accompaniment.

"AIII AHHH UH UH UH *UHHHH*," moaned Miss Jungle Fever.

Callie makes a few Chiquita Banana motions with her hands which degenerate into wrings.

"COME ON DOWN TO SPANISH HAR-LAAAAM . . ." (two three bump, one two three bump. Bump.)

Next time around she'll hit the card of someone like red freak Toni, asymmetrical, spacy music like "D.O.A." and Jimi Hendrix. For these she switched to something that looked like the first class in modern-dance gym: "A few basic motions expressing how you really *feel*, girls, no, Callie dear, I mean not the way you *think* a dancer should move, but an organic flow. I don't care if it's clumsy or awkward, I just want it to be real. Good, Callie, excellent, that certainly looks real. . . ."

"I'M A COMINA *GITCHA* . . ." promised Jimi, as Callie fluttered earnestly.

Meanwhile she was doing something very strange. She was listening to the music. I mean stopping dead in the middle of a dance and standing there, head to one side. In the break between songs she commented to the audience, "I loved the key change in the middle . . ." "That's nice the way they stop everything but the drum . . ."

"Jesus, what a ring-a-ding," said the manager, shaking his head.

Behind the bar was the same story. It's hard to fuck up on a metered tap. The beer starts and stops automatically, and all the girl does is hold a glass and push a button. It takes a while, though, to learn to pour a good beer, as I found out the few times I tried, and nobody blamed Callie for beers that were three quarters foam except the customers, who wouldn't take them. Callie, all pardons, dumped the beer down the drain and pulled another disaster out of the tap. Well, a girl's first few nights—patience.

She also, however, had a strange habit of holding the mug under the tap upside down. There she stands, doubled over the tap, seventy-five cents worth of beer she's going to end up paying for sloshing over the wrong end of the mug, her large butt entirely blocking the aisle, with the girls shouting "Fuck! shit! piss!" piled up on either side of her, and she's saying, "Oh, my goodness, not again!"

Yes, and there's Callie at the register, counting change for a ten—"Four, five, six, seven, eight, eleven, twelve . . ." while the girls with drawers above and below her wave fists full of bills and a customer bangs his glass, although he will very soon be delighted to receive for his ten-spot eighteen dollars in change.

She redeemed herself at the bar, though, by washing most of the mugs singlehanded. She'd been told that part of the job was collecting and washing the empties; she didn't seem to realize this was a shared effort, and none of the girls was about to enlighten her, either. So there's Callie with her rump sticking out the other way this time, carefully rubbing and rinsing each mug separately, until someone who needs a batch of glasses shoves her out of the way, grabs four mugs in each hand, sloshes them through the three sinks in one continuous motion, and bangs them down on the drainboard with a dirty look.

"That's clever," smiles Callie and gets back to work.

Out on the floor the big backside also protruded, with predictable results, as Callie, her nose practically in some guy's lap, tried to reason the dude into letting her go. An experienced dancer knows more moves and countermoves than a Kung Fu master; Callie was constantly getting pinioned.

Between one thing and another, she didn't sell much beer, and with all those spills and making wrong change and getting ripped off for twenty-five dollars in the dressing room, I think that first week she ended up paying Obie's more than Obie's paid her.

There was more to it than inexperience or clumsiness, however. Either she was actually retarded or too smart for the job, thinking when she should have been on automatic pilot.

There was also the way she walked right into empty tables and then begged their pardon . . . the way she always missed the last step . . . the upside-down mugs . . . the way she sat down on things that weren't there . . . the way, one night when the Buzzer went off, she ran into the door marked MEN . . .

Sure enough, I saw her one night in the car putting on a pair of very thick glasses.

But, I remember thinking, it's not only because

My week was up. I got my checks and told Whitey I was cutting out. He gave me a couple of joints for the road and told me to drop by when I was down this way again.

Paula kissed me on the mouth and said, "Jethuth, Petey, I'm thorry you're leaving."

I wasn't, not when I left the motel for the last time the next morning, and the sun was shining, and I realized I hadn't been out of bed before noon for a whole month.

I walked to the freeway and stuck out my thumb. A car of well-dressed chicks passed; one of them smiled at me apologetically. Instead of seeing girls I saw prospective bottomless dancers. I wondered how they'd hack dropping their pants for the first time, how they'd do up there, how . . .

Hell, it was high time I got out of that place. Obie's was becoming real to me, and the rest of it unnatural, as if sunshine and birds and girls who smiled for real were a novelty you paid to get into for a few hours to escape from that dark and permanent reality.

My nights off, for instance. The first night I went to

a movie. It got out at ten-thirty. I went and had a hamburger at Denny's, then I headed straight back to the bar and sat there till closing time.

What do you do in a strange town? I don't get off much on movies. I didn't know anybody. The only thing I'm used to doing with my spare time is practice the violin.

My next night off I went to the library. I figured I'd get a few books for the afternoons I spent lying on my bed, for the slow times by the door. It was a good old-fashioned library, the kind of building that makes me think of the 1930s, high ceilings, marble, brass banisters, heavy oak tables. A few people moved quietly around in the respectful heel-toe pad induced by echoing stone floors. The acoustics in that great old vault were terrific. Everyone whispered. Conversations were a soothing, cloisteral resonance of murmurs against the larger silence.

I spent five nights a week under an amplifier, surrounded by howling, bopping maniacs; at the library I'd come home.

I spent two more evenings there, and then, one night, I got the feeling people were avoiding my table. Suddenly I was convinced it was the smell. That Obie's smell. After the first impact when you got there, you stopped noticing it. You were saturated, the whole place was saturated, there was no contrast. But wake up the next day and the pillow your head had been on stank, the clothes on the floor reeked.

I kept aside a shirt and a pair of jeans I never wore to the bar—my civies—and I washed my hair every day, even when I'd only be right back in it a few hours later.

Still, I missed things. I'd be out on the street,

walking along, and suddenly get a whiff of that unmistakable odor. I'd look all around, run through my pockets, and finally discover it was my comb—I had loaned it to a dancer the night before to pull through her sweaty hair.

I kept smelling that sour carpet smell, and I got a little frantic until I found it was my shoes. The seams along the bottoms of my shoes were all gummed up with ooze; the uppers were beginning to separate.

I got so freaked out I even bought some male cologne and doused myself before I went out.

Still I began to feel, there in the library, that people were avoiding me because of the smell. Maybe I was getting so used to it I couldn't even smell it on the outside any more. It was becoming a part of me, something no scrubbing or perfume could get rid of, like those ancient Egyptians who worked in the House of the Dead embalming corpses and who became so permeated with the chemicals they used that people couldn't stand being near them, and they were locked permanently into their dead society deep in the steaming caverns, where only the lowest, most wretched whores came, and a fresh young female corpse was pumped full of other than embalming fluids.

Worse yet. I was sitting alone at my table one night when suddenly the murmurs changed. The soothing drone was breaking up into sets of vowels. Aii uh ahahahah uhhhh. Good God, it's "Jungle Fever!"

I look around, ready to jump on the moron with the transistor radio. Either that or some high-school stud doing what I once did with the third violin in my high-school orchestra—I was concert master, which is probably what induced her to let things go so far—in the S section of the stacks. At some point she grabbed compulsively at a shelf and buried us in *Cannery Rows*.

My eyes light on a woman stretching for a book and . . . I have X-ray eyes! Suddenly, the X-ray eyes, right in the San Jose Public Library.

The gray-haired librarian with the toothy smile is shaking her withered dugs at me. The teenybopper in jeans reading on the floor is spreading her cunt for that old duffer holding *Horticulture News*. I know you, you old goat, sitting there in your bifocals, pretending to be a kindly and slightly senile lover of flowers. I've seen your eyes turn neon in the red darkness. I've seen you courting cardiac arrest from fourteen different angles. I'm reporting you to Medi-Cal. Jesus.

Yes, high time for young Peter Stern to hit the road. I can tell Robert about this and we'll laugh. My month as doorman in a bottomless joint.

I got a lift with a guy going to Berkeley. He had A.M. radio, and every third song was right off our jukebox.

We got to Berkeley around eleven. I decided there was no rush and got myself some coffee at an outdoor café near the University. The sun was shining and the freaks were blooming and the sky was very blue. I sat in the sun feeling happy and liberated.

I found myself thinking about Mexico. I was finally free from all that too. Mother had passed on to some ultimate frangipani haven. She wasn't around any more, either to please or accuse. It had all ended in that bar in Acapulco.

I was twelve and feeling sick—Mother kept urging sips of her drink on me. "Come on, kiddo, farewell celebration"—joking a lot with the bartender, showing off for both of us: "See, I bet you didn't imagine I had such a big boy," and "See, down here I am surrounded by friends, I have a happy life."

She still wore her wedding ring, and the publicity photograph in the glass case in the lobby, retouched by somebody with the eye of a mortician, said AT THE GOLDEN PIANO, MISS HAZEL STERN.

Mother made a point to explain that she'd only kept the name because there was a well-known band leader named Sammy Stern, and it wouldn't do her career any harm if people associated them.

Sammy Stern! How the mighty had fallen. At those Sunday afternoon children's concerts Mother used to drag me to, along with all the other pale, overdisciplined twits, she always had me take my violin in its little three-quarter case, and when we got to the box office she'd yell "Stern" as she handed in our passes so maybe someone would think we were related to Isaac.

Is that why she married my father? Because there was no one named Heifetz or Menuhin around?

When I was nine I came home from school one day and both the pianos were gone, the Steinway I'd sat under ever since I was a baby, spacing out on the reverberations, and the Baldwin Mother used for her pupils. What struck me most were the hollows of clean carpet where the legs had been.

When I saw her three years later I didn't recognize my mother. Her skin had roughened in the sun like hide. She seemed to have thickened and shrunk: "The last time I saw this kid of mine he was up to here," Mother announced to one and all, indicating a leathery bosom. "Now he can eat peanuts off the top of my head."

She went in for serapes and hat-dance hats and yards of skirt with things like real dried starfish netted into them. At night she wore low-cut blouses that showed off an embalmed-looking cleavage.

"People out drinking don't just want to listen. They want to look. You're a package."

She even talked differently, like a nun's idea of show biz: "Well, chum, what do you think of your old Mommy now—quite a change, huh, kiddo?"

The only thing the same was the eyes, the greenest eyes in the world. Mother had the unclouded eyes of a young girl. Her music, the music I grew up with, was like her eyes. Pure, narrow, wistful, lonely.

One afternoon Mother took me along to an auditorium with acoustics like a roller rink where she accompanied rehearsals of a musical called *In Gay Acapulco*. She did this several times a week for free with the understanding she'd be right in there when the show made the big time.

As Mother grimly banged out something called "Enchilada Lotta's Gotta Lotta Love to Give Ya," a wild-eyed young man waiting for his turn made sounds like pigs and donkeys on the violin for my amusement. I didn't tell him I played.

Afterward, Mother introduced me to the producers, two silvery dudes named Rodney Fern and Forbes Manly—I never forgot those names—who thought I was lucky to have such a wonderful and talented mother. For a moment Rodney and Forbes linked arms across Mother's heavy shoulders. Mother beamed, and even the sunshine seemed part of some elaborate justification ceremony to which I politely acceded, swallowing the question I kept wanting to ask the whole time I was there: "Why didn't you take me with you, Mother? Why the hell did you walk out on me?"

One night Mother switched in mid cha-cha to the

finale of a Chopin ballad. When she finished, a man put a dollar bill in the tip glass on top of the piano and walked out. During her break Mother explained how this guy first walked in the bar a few months ago, and despite the years she recognized him instantly. This was a boy a few years ahead of her at Juilliard, the pride of the school, a runner-up in the Levintritt at the age of eighteen. In the competition he played the Chopin Ballad in G Minor.

Thirty years later, a trembling wreck, he turns up in a bar in Acapulco, and Mother, recalling with ghoulish accuracy, dashed off a few bars just to see what would happen.

"It was amazing," said Mother proudly. "He got up, walked a few steps, and collapsed! They all thought he was drunk."

Later he poured out to Mother the series of tragedies that had killed his music. Now he came to the bar once or twice a month for Mother to salt his wounds with arpeggios.

Pretty precocious musically at twelve, if totally backward in other ways, I wondered even then what deafness or rot had afflicted two graduates of the best music school in the country. Mother made the Chopin sound like "Smoke Gets in Your Eyes." Evidently the sloppy, flashy style she cultivated for the golden piano was the only style she had left now.

One night while the Mexican comedian who alternated sets with her was up there convulsing the tourists, Mother looked at the ceiling and said, "You're getting old enough to understand these things, Peter—you might as well know that with your father it was just in-and-out. Never any tenderness. Just in-and-out."

I was the only person in the bar who wasn't

laughing at the comedian, precisely because I didn't understand about in-and-out, though I had some rather baroque theories. I didn't really get what Mother meant until much later, back home again with old In-and-Out himself, and then I was embarrassed for all three of us, especially that poor dumb twelve-year-old in the bar.

Later still, after I found out firsthand about in-and-out, I remembered the music I had heard sitting under the Steinway, that lonely, unripe flood, and realized Mother had spent her life a virgin, never reached, never grown up, till the firmness had gone rigid and the passion all surface and a bulky stranger closed over her like a scar.

After the visit, we wrote letters that said nothing, with decreasing frequency. I hadn't written for a year the summer I blew it with a chick I really wanted, the girl named Linda I lived with all the sunny months, and decided the things that needed sorting out in me should begin by asking Mother that question I never asked her when I was twelve. But Mother was gone without a word—which was in a way its own answer.

The University bells rang the noon. I got up and started walking down toward the freeway.

For the second time, I don't know why I did it. Maybe thinking about the bar in Acapulco. Maybe thinking about why people run out on things. Maybe, even back then, Callie. Whatever it was, when I got to the end of University Avenue and found a fellow hitcher's discarded sign that said SOUTH, I took it as an omen and held it out and got back to San Jose in time to catch a nap before the night shift.

It was almost three in the morning and we were sitting in Leroy's Café—me, Callie, Fat Mary, and Miss R.H.—having breakfast. There's a Denny's a few blocks in the other direction, and some of the girls prefer that, but I went there once with a couple and came out feeling like a cheap pimp among the plaid jackets and plastic coiffures jet-setting it in Denny's at three a.m. of a San Jose morning.

At Leroy's, among the truck drivers and hardhats doing graveyard shifts, we were the jet set, the impressario and his golden girls.

It was the first night Callie was spending time with anybody from the club, and now only because she had to wait for Libby, who was having breakfast with Gerry at Denny's, and preferred, by a slight margin, our company to sitting in a cold car with drunks beating on the locked windows in the parking lot at Obie's.

Not that Callie wasn't friendly enough. She always had that big shy smile for me when she walked in to work, and she was always happy to punch someone's music for them, switch sets with a girl who needed a break, bring the dancer a glass of water, come up with a safety pin or an emergency Tampax.

But she never hung around in the office either when the banks were all counted and the money was sitting on the desk in piles with rubber bands around them and everyone laughing and jiving, spaced out on hits of the evening's hysteria that hung around the bar in pockets, like tear gas. She didn't hang around in the dressing room while the girls sat around on empty beer kegs discussing life. She and Libby came together and left together in a big old yellow DeSoto. During the evening they stuck close. No old men ever dropped them off or picked them up, but they had politely declined dates with two managers, three doormen, Slate, and Gerry.

"Hey, what's with those two chicks?" the manager asked me, snapping his gum. "You think they're Lesbies?"

It didn't seem likely now that Libby had gone off with Gerry, also giving us a chance to clear up some other questions.

Fat Mary didn't waste any time. As soon as we had ordered she said to Callie, "You know, my pussy been tickling all night, hee hee," and dramatized with a hand under the table.

Callie smiled politely.

Having established rapport, Mary plunged right in.

"Say, where you come from anyhow."

"San Francisco," Callie smiled.

"That right? I got a old man live in San Francisco. Would you happen to know a cat named George who lives on Sixth Avenue over by the park there? He's a dealer, but don't say I said so."

"I haven't lived there for quite a few years. I'm afraid not."

"O.K., where you live now?"

"Berkeley."

"You don't talk much, do you. You doing a heavy red scene or something?"

"Oh, no. I mean yes. I talk. Where do *you* come from?"

"Here, there, and everywhere," said Fat Mary, abandoning geography as a line of inquiry. "Say, can I ask you something? Why do you do that to your hair? You got something against your head?"

Callie ran a hand over her hair. The corkscrews withdrew and popped up again behind her hand like feelers after a heavy footstep.

"I've always worn my hair like this. Otherwise it's terribly—kinky, you see."

Simultaneously she registered Fat Mary's headful of kinks.

Conversation waned.

Miss R.H. stepped into the breach.

"Why don't you get a fall?" she croaked. "You'd look good in a fall."

"What's a fall?" said Callie.

"She don't need no fall," said Fat Mary crossly. "You take my advice you get a good cut and shape. I bet you look almost as good as Angela Davis."

"While you're at it, why don't you get yourself a decent costume?"

"You know, this is really quite tasty," said Callie, addressing a sausage.

Mary and Miss R.H. looked at each other. We ate in silence for a while.

Leroy brought the bill and the girls brought out their dollars and quarters. Tip money.

"You know something funny?" said Fat Mary,

sipping her coffee. "About three weeks ago some-body ripped off a scuzzy old pair of shoes I had out of the dressing room, and tonight they was *back*. Guess they pinched whoever ripped them off just like they pinched me."

"I wish someone would do that with my twenty-five dollars," said Callie.

"Forget that. Where money's concerned, you can't trust *no one* in that place. Why, honey, I meet my grandmother working in that place, I rip off her Social Security, and she better not leave her teeth lying around, neither. You just got watch everybody like a hawk. Say, can I ask you something else? How much you make in tips?"

"Tonight I made ten-fifty—no, eleven, but then I was short five dollars. Oh, I could have cried."

"What do you make on a *good* night?"

"This is the best night I've had since I started. Why?"

"It figures. The way you spend all that time rapping with the dudes, and washing glasses—I bet you the only bottomless dancer who comes home from work with dishpan hands. You want to know how much I made in tips tonight? And it's Tuesday, right? Meaning things are slow. Tonight I made thirty-four dollars. On a weekend I never walk out with less than fifty."

"Fifty dollars! My goodness, how do you do it?"

"I hustle my ass off, that's how. I pop a few whites and I *go*. You got to remember there's two, three other girls out there will run over their own mothers getting to the door. So you really got to hustle. When you get down off that stage, don't take no half hour buckling things up and fanning yourself. You get yourself a pair of stretch underwear like I got, slips on and off real easy, and you hit that floor hustling. You want to catch the guys just wet their pants over you, they more likely to leave you the quarter. And stop being so fucking dainty. I personally beat your ass about ten times tonight because you're asking can you get the dude a beer and I'm standing there with the beer in my hand ready to lay it on him. Don't ask him do he want the beer! He *got* to want it. That's what it says over the door, one beer minimum, if he ain't going for it he can talk to the man. I always got a beer in my hand and a tip tray and some quarters, so I don't have to run back and forth to the register all the time. I'm not giving myself a hernia for *no* fucking dive!"

"Always use a tip tray," croaked Miss R.H.

"That's right. The dude, he'll take the quarter out of your hand, but the tray makes him stop and think. Then you make it hard for him. He hold out his hand for you to slide the money off the tray, just stand there looking dumb. Don't never just leave the tray on the table. Hang on to it until he take the change or he leave it. You hold it just far enough away, he got to stretch a little to get at the money."

"Don't waste the effort on pool players. They always need the quarter for the table."

"That's right. Never waste no time over pool players. Now I'm going to show you what I'm talking about."

Fat Mary got one of the brown restaurant trays from the end of the counter. She put a quarter on it.

"This here is our typical dude"—she held the tray out toward me; I leered obligingly and made a grab at her ass—"and I am bringing him his change. I hold the tray right about here, and I yell good and loud, so if he takes it anyhow all his friends know he is a cheap bastard: 'HERE'S YOUR CHANGE, LOVER.' "

There was no jukebox at Leroy's to drown out the sound. Ten hardhats turned around to look.

"If he's a young guy call him 'sir,' " added Miss R.H. "It's worth twenty-five cents to a young guy just to have someone in their panties call him sir."

"I always call the old ones 'stud.' They really get off on that, hee hee. Right in the hearing aid: 'HERE'S YOUR CHANGE, STUD.' "

I reached for Mary's quarter. I couldn't get any purchase on it.

"See what I'm doing? I hold the tray a little off the table, and every time he try to pry that quarter up I let my wrist go sort of limp. If we was at the bar I'd rub some slops on the tray, it gives the quarter more traction. Meanwhile I'm standing right between him and the stage so he can't see nothing, and I sort of got my armpit in his nose. Pretty soon he got to be a real hard case if he don't give up on the whole thing."

Leroy brought our change on one of the trays.

"You ever try a thin film of mashed potatoes?" he said.

I asked Callie if she could give me a lift on her way to Denny's; home was now a flea pit on First Avenue, which I figured was at least an occasional change of milieu.

We got into the DeSoto. Callie drove the way she danced, jerking and grinding the whole way.

"I just passed my driver's test last week," she apologized.

"Would you satisfy my curiosity? Is it flower or dog?"

"I beg your pardon?"

"Your name."

"Oh, I see. Neither, really. It's pee."

"Pee?"

"Callio*pe*."

"Calliope! She was one of the Muses, wasn't she. What is it, dance, drama . . . ?"

"I'm surprised you know about Muses at all. Somehow one doesn't expect people at Obie's to know things like that."

I received a hard look that resulted in a missed stop sign. I decided it had better wait till we'd stopped.

"Is this where you *live?*"

"This is the place," I said, trying to sound like it was gay and eccentric to live in a place called Toomy's Transient Hotel. "Like to see the accommodations?"

"Thank you. Libby is probably waiting, and we have a long drive ahead of us."

"You live in Berkeley, you said?"

"Yes."

"Do you drive home every night?"

"Yes, we do."

"That's a pretty long haul."

"It's not so bad. We share the driving."

"Wouldn't it be easier if you stayed over one or two nights? I mean share a motel room or something?"

"I couldn't do that. I have two kids to look after in the morning. And a husband."

That, obviously, was that. But I couldn't leave it alone. Suavely: "May I say you look mighty young for two kids."

"Not really. I'll be thirty-five on my next birthday."

She stared me straight in the eye.

That, young Mr. Stern, really is that.

I got out of the car and watched a thirty-five-year-old bottomless dancing mother of two named Calliope bump off into the night.

Nine-forty-five at night, a good house, everyone drinking up. It's the end of a good week, breaking a thousand every night. The manager is happy. He has survived another week of Obie's pressure cooker "Crack a thousand or start looking for another job"; he has been favored by the phases of the moon, or the temperature, or the stock market, or the world situation, whatever it is that brings the customers in cycles so marked you'll spend weeks with ten dudes in the bar all night and suddenly be packing them in like sardines.

So he's gotten a little loose, he's drinking beer and playing pool, and that means everyone else is a little loose, including me, taking advantage of a lull at the door to get on with this week's doorman book, Dante's *Inferno*.

Suddenly I look up and, Jesus God! it's our local police, the ones who drop in whenever things get dull on the beat. I was so engrossed they'd got all the way inside the door without my noticing.

My heart started thumping. A bust cost Obie a lot of bread. The girls have to get paid even when they're sitting on their asses in the police station, plus paying the girls who take over, and bail, and all the while losing money on the dudes who scram and the ones who don't come in because we're short dancers. It's bad enough when it can't be helped, but when it's somebody's fault heads start to roll.

The cops looked a little embarrassed about the whole thing. The older one reached over me apologetically and pressed the Buzzer.

Sure, it was a game, but there were rules. If your pawn gets to square nine it can't not become a queen. So they had to arrest somebody.

Callie, up on stage, didn't even have a chance to grab her costume.

Whitey ran out of the office screaming, because losing a girl tonight would be a real disaster. There were only two girls beside Callie working, another dancer and a beer-seller; as often happened, the two other scheduled dancers just hadn't shown up for work.

"I mean shit!" Whitey was yelling. "You guys rounded up every girl I had just two nights ago. How often does this have to go on?"

Apologetically, the cops arrested Whitey.

Callie, looking dazed, walked past followed by the younger cop. I grabbed her hand and gave it a squeeze.

"I don't believe this," she murmured and marched off to the police car.

Slate took over the door. I went into the office with Joe.

"We are in real trouble," he said. "Me and Whitey called every girl in the book just an hour ago when the agency chicks didn't show. I even fired two of them right over the phone because they wouldn't get out of bed. You got any girl friends?"

Rudy, one of our regulars, stuck his head in the door.

"Cyndi says to tell you she's been dancing for half an hour and she's only doing one more song."

"Tell her she dances till I say stop. Go tell that beer-seller to get her ass in here."

The beer-seller came in, a dumpy, sweet-faced creature in nylon baby dolls.

"You're Lynn, right?"

"Karen."

"That's right. Lynn's the other one. Okay, Karen, after Cyndi finishes this song I want you to go up there and dance a few songs. You don't have to take anything off, just to give Cyndi a break, let her sell some beer."

Karen shook her head.

"I don't dance."

"Come on, everybody dances. I don't care what it looks like, just get up there and keep the stage occupied while we work on getting another dancer."

Karen shook her head again.

"It's no big thing. Just do me a favor. Look, just to be nice I'll pay you three for the rest of the night."

Beer-sellers got a buck seventy-five an hour, as opposed to the dancers' four, for running around all night in a bathing suit. It was supposed to be worth it for the tips, but even so this chick must have really had something against dancing. She shook her head again.

"Okay, now I'm not asking you. Go up and dance, or put your clothes on and go home and don't come back."

It was an empty threat—what would he do with one dancer and *no* beer-seller—but Karen didn't look quite bright enough to work that out. She gave him a very soulful look and walked out.

While Karen was cringing up on stage to boos and screams of "TAKE IT OFF!" Paula squealed into the parking lot like a race driver.

"Whitey called me from the station," she said. "I'm here to help out."

She was ring-eyed and rumpled, like she'd just got out of bed. I supposed she could wash some glasses, but I didn't know what good she could do otherwise, unless she had some private source of dancers.

Maybe she did, because a few minutes later I walked out of the office and instead of Karen there was a gorgeous blonde up there in a hot pink bikini and high black spikes with a twist of pearls and platinum half way down her back. Silver and pink and black against a deep tan.

Goddam, it *was*.

Paula.

Never mind the magic of the lights and the make-up. There was more going for her up there than that. Miss R.H. had the wig and the paint and the trips too, but what Paula had was coming from inside, and the guys were delirious, clapping and stamping over a fifty-year-old broad who didn't even take her top off.

Naturally they tried to make her, but Paula kept them quiet for five minutes just taking off her ring, sliding it verrrrry slowly up her finger, then at the tip sliding it back down, and up, and down, and up down updown updown updownupdownupdown, with the guys humping and clapping in rhythm.

"TAKE IT OFF!" yelled some diehard, and Paula, in mid-song, stopped and walked to the front of the stage, put her hands on her hips, looked right down at the guy, and said, "Nah, I'm too old. My boobs retired last year. Now the right one's on Medical and the left one's living in a trailer in Arizona," and proceeded to do ten minutes of yoga exercises, standing on her head, folding up like an accordion with her toes next to her ears, some incredibly limber shit. When she sensed she was pushing it too far, she got up, gave two high kicks and a bow and ran down to clapping and cheers, leaving the stage to Cyndi's bare and prosaic expanses. The timing was perfect. Naked as a bluejay, twenty-two years old, Cyndi got no more than a few whistles.

Paula alternated sets with Cyndi and Karen all night. When she wasn't dancing she helped with the glasses and sat rapping with the dudes. Pretty soon when she went up they'd start chanting.

"PAUL-A! PAUL-A! PAUL-A!"

I finally figured it out. Enjoyment. Paula was enjoying dancing. Paula was enjoying the dudes. Paula enjoyed Paula. It's the same thing whatever's happening—a violinist enjoying his music, a teacher enjoying what he's teaching, a baseball player enjoying his game. The joy, not the medium, is the biggest turn-on for whoever's watching.

I also decided that Paula's age might even be an advantage. At least half our customers were over forty themselves. Young chicks are far out to watch, but give the dudes a still very fuckable woman who had also been where they'd been, knew the score, could *understand*—I think that if their wives had turned out like Paula they probably wouldn't be here in the first place.

The manager topped his thousand again, which, considering the bust, gave him lots of points. My role in the mess just slid on by.

Paula came out of the dressing room.

"Well, howdy, stranger," she said to me. "How's things at the old Crusted Arms."

"I've been meaning to drop around the motel."

"Never mind. I know how it is. You're all the same. Good old Paula, fine when you need her. Take Whitey. I haven't even heard his voice on the telephone for over a week, then suddenly it's, "Hey, Ma, I'm in jail, start dancing.""

"What's going on down there anyhow?" I said, suddenly reminded. So totally does Obie's close over any gaps in its dark continuum that once people leave it's like they never existed.

"If they're not out by now, it means they're spending the night. Don't worry about it. Whitey can take care of himself. What are you worried about? Miss Goody Two Boobs? She'll live. Want to get some breakfast?"

In the car she said, "We better go to Leroy's. Gerry does his courting at Denny's and I don't want to cramp his style."

I'd been wondering if that topic was mentionable. Now that Paula had brought it up herself I said what I was thinking: "You're being pretty broad-minded about that."

"Me? You should have known me when, kid. When I have something to hang onto, I'm murder. Somebody fools with my old man, I'll cut her gizzard out. If you want to keep an old man in this business you have to take a hard line. There's lots of pretty bodies around with a lot of fucked-up heads attached to them. But Gerry—there's nothing there to hold on to. It's not his fault. When God was handing out hearts Gerry just happened to get a little one. I'm perfectly satisfied to get my bed warmed every once in a while. Listen, I figure I'm doing a lot of people a favor letting that dumb puppy into my bedroom. At least now the chicks he seduces have a chance to learn to like it before they go around spreading the word. You multiply the amount of joy one good stud can pass on, I bet a dozen of them in good condition could change the world. Speaking of which, how have things been with you? How come you're hanging around loose at two in the morning? Don't you got some little dancer yet waiting up with a nice plate of hot lasagne?"

We pulled in to Leroy's.

"Jesus, I can't even get out of the car. My knees are on fire. I must be getting too old. Give me a hand."

Paula limped inside on my arm.

"You know, Paula, before tonight I didn't even know you were a dancer."

"You didn't, huh? That's my son again. Every blue moon when there's some emergency he remembers I'm a dancer. Otherwise I'm just the person who scrambles eggs for him and his friends at three in the morning. Well, it must be my fault somewhere he turned out so selfish. I guess I deserve it. Tell me your mother doesn't spoil you rotten."

I told her.

"You mean you don't even know where she is? Jesus, Petey, that's a bummer. You know that's one thing I'll never understand. I'm a dancer. I was a dancer when those kids over at the club were making poo-poo in their diapers, and believe me, when you're a dancer you see everything. Vice, per-version—listen, I worked at one club where most of the girls weren't girls, you know what I mean? I used to help them tape their cocks into their asses. I mean what the hell. I had a real thing for one of those guys, but he couldn't handle it. He was afraid digging a chick meant he was turning Lesbian. Don't smile. I've been in more than one bar with the ambulance and the stretcher with the blanket hanging down over the sides. The manager mops up the blood and you keep dancing. I can understand a lot—people get scared or lonely or pissed off—but there's one thing I never can understand, and that's a mother who runs out on her kids. It's the most basic instinct there is—you stand by those kids. Steal for them, kill for them, whore for them, right on. But leave them—excuse me, Petey, maybe your mother had her reasons, and maybe I should shut my big mouth."

"It's O.K., Paula, I'm interested."

"Understand, Petey, I'm not saying I can't see the temptation. When my first husband told me he was very sorry but he couldn't take the feeling of being tied down, I was eighteen years old. Ralphie was what—a year old, and I was pregnant with Whitey. What's an eighteen-year-old girl like? I wanted lots of fun and lots of boy friends, and what I got was lots of shitty diapers and nights trapped in with two screaming babies. It wasn't like today. Today it's hip to have a baby, you carry it around on your back in one of those little things, and all the boys with long hair think it's organic. In my day, if you were a woman alone with a kid it meant all you thought about was getting some dude to play Papa and foot the bills. When men found out you had a kid it was bye-bye baby. I used to hire some high-school girl to baby-sit, and go down to a bar and when it was twelve o'clock I'd lie my head off about why I had to get home. I tell you I wanted to strangle those kids. I wanted to put them in the car and drive somewhere deserted and just walk away. Leaving them in a basket in front of some church was too good for the way I felt about babies. When that bastard split he left me a hundred fifty dollars. When that ran out, I didn't even know how I was going to feed them. I started answering ads, but there wasn't much I knew how to do. Finally I went to this one for a cocktail waitress, and the dude looks me over and says can you dance, and I say no, and that's that. I go home and my little boy is crying, he's hungry and there's no food in the goddam cuboard. I went right back to that place and said, "Can I dance!" and by God I got up there and danced. That, by the way, was the beginning of my dancing career. I sewed a lot of ruffles on a one-piece bathing suit, and I was still dancing on my way to the hospital. Whitey was two months early and that's why. Jesus, you never saw anything so small in your life. I guess that's why I let him get away with so much now. He was so little, and I was so scared he was going to die."

Paula stopped, thinking about it.

"How'd you meet Obie?"

"How else? I was working at one of his clubs. Salinas, can you believe it? Mothers hid their children's eyes when I walked by. No shit! In those days being a dancer was like being a whore. Nowadays they got dancing college professors and topless lawyers, it's just another trip. In my day when I wheeled my baby carriage into the playground they all moved over to the other side like I had cancer. It was heavy. Maybe I shouldn't be such a wise-ass. Maybe if Obie hadn't come along I would have ended up flipping out and dumping them. I can say plenty against Obie, but one thing you got to give him, he's a prince with kids. To this day—divorces, new wives, new husbands, the bit—he's still doing it. He's got Robert managing Burlingame and San Matteo, and Whitey's working with him down here. Gerry! Gerry's just a good-looking punk from nowhere, drifts on up here, Obie likes him and now he's teaching him the muscle end of the business. If it happens to be a chick, Obie puts the make on her. So he's a dirty old man. I guess Gerry makes me a dirty old woman. I still have the feeling me and Obie will end up together in some old-age home, throwing crutches at each other. But Jesus, was I mad at that fucker when he turned this bar bottomless! This used to be a nice bar to come to, a nice mellow place. These were the days when the Animal Shelter was still next door, and the guys used to come over from there with little kittens buttoned up inside their jackets and things. But what are you going to do? Bottomless is a fact. It's real. It's there. It exists, like it or not. I guess there's nothing wrong with bottomless. Shit, it's natural. Don't we all come into this world bottomless? It's the clubs that make it stink—the managers and the owners. They treat the girls like animals. For a long time I wanted to open my own bar. I would have run a real clean place. But I'm too lazy. I'd rather sit around and bitch. Listen, Petey, I didn't mean to come down on your mother like that. I'm sure she loves you. Maybe it's just something like being sick, something you can't help. You just remember, you ever need someone to fry an egg in the middle of the night, the motel's open twenty-four hours. That's my problem. I haven't got enough young punks taking advantage of me."

Libby and Gerry were obviously doing a number. They huddled together all over the bar. Libby started waiting around at night and left with Gerry in his GTO. Callie drove off by herself in Libby's car.

Now Libby was dancing for somebody, not just her own crackled image in the mirror. She still did her thumper rabbit dance, but it stopped being such a solemn exercise. She giggled and did little pantomime routines—it's hot, I'm tired, hello down there.

Occasionally Gerry sat down and watched her, legs sprawled, the king of the heap, the guy who had access to that coveted little item. Gerry, a fancy dresser, particularly went in for far-out ties which he wore loosened in the open neck of an immaculate shirt and somehow managed to keep casually flipped over his shoulder at all times: young man on the go. Actually there wasn't much for him to do at the bar, and he spent most of the night playing pool or lounging in the office twirling his gun.

Gerry had a lot of dark, curly hair he had a habit of tossing back from his forehead. His skin was olive and he wore a little beard and mustache; his lips were very full and red against the dark hair. He was a handsome bastard and Libby acted stoked out of her mind.

"Whew!" she said happily, "I can smell my cunt every time I take my pants off up there."

Young love at Obie's.

Libra Lou, however, was in for trouble.

One night a woman about Paula's age showed up. She was wearing a sort of soft, oatmealy suit, pearls around the neck, and she was driving a Mercedes.

A variety of females crashed this male bailiwick, but I'd never seen one like this before, and never alone. In fact, the only woman who ever came alone to Obie's was a lieutenant in the Vice Squad, who, when she wasn't checking out go-go bars, hung around street corners pretending to be a prostitute. Whenever she showed up the whispers scuttled from dancer to dancer: "Don't touch yourself. It's the Vice ... the Vice ... the Vice ..."

Aside from being busted for general nakedness, the girls could get arrested for indecent behavior or lewd public display, some weird category like that. For this offense Obie's won't go bail, considering its responsibility ended by hanging a list in the office.

DANCERS MUST NOT
1   Touch any part of their body and/or genitalia
2   Engage in any act involving touching each other's breasts and/or genitalia
3   Approach any customer closer than six feet with exposed breasts and/or genitalia
4   The breasts and/or genitalia must be covered at all times when dancer is not on stage

No Lude Dancing. Always Ware Costumze offstage.

The last two admonitions had been added in pen by some manager.

Not counting the lieutenant, dancers, hookers, and managers' old ladies, maybe three or four chicks a night passed my portals. They usually came in a group, two guys with the chicks hanging very tight to their arms, a kooky thing to do on a double date, but now they're actually inside it seems so weird—*cheap*—so disgusting. They close their eyes and hang on tight.

Sometimes the women are older and straight-looking, stockings, glasses, on the arms of their bald, beady-eyed husbands. What do they get out of this? Which one wanted to come? What's the guy doing here with his *wife?*

Wives are a bad joke at Obie's.

"There's someone outside looking for a Bill Wilson," Slate shouts.

"It's your wife, Billy!" some wiseguy yells.

"With a baseball bat!" yells somebody else.

"And a big black boy friend!" adds another.

All the escaped husbands laugh and go back to their fantasies of bedding the dancer, except for this dummy who, not to speak of having to keep his hands off himself, has right next to him a varicose reminder of what really awaits him.

The ladies sit stiffly with their legs sagging at the ankles and sad eyes, watching all that young flesh, watching the old man watch it. But at least they have the consolation of the shiny head and the paunch; it's not likely the old buzzard will ever get any of that action.

It's harder on the chicks with healthy young studs. Stranger things have happened than running off with a bottomless dancer from San Jose. How is the young lady to know that her own grandmother, even with her teeth ripped off, could activate a few weiners up there under the rosy lights?

Every once in a while one of these young chicks gets desperate or drunk enough and runs up on stage next to the dancer. Suddenly you realize how mechanical the dancers are with one of these chicks next to them, eyes screwed shut in embarrassment, dancing for dear life.

She pulls off her clothes like a person stripping to jump in after someone who's drowning. The customers strain forward. Goddam, at Obie's you forget that there really is something strong and awesome in a woman exposing her body for a crowd of strangers.

She finally gets her pants off. The men cheer and whistle. She relaxes, opens her eyes, smiles. It's like an orgasm. She's done it! He likes bottomless dancers? O.K., now he's got one.

But most of the time the chicks stay in their seats, hanging tight to their guys, hands all over him—hey, dig, this is *mine*—and she smiles brightly at the dancer who brings him his beer, trying hard not to get defeated by it all.

There's only one type of lady who actually seems to enjoy herself. A couple once offered Fat Mary ten dollars to let them stick their fingers up her in the girls' room.

"I go, ten *dollars?* Honey, for ten dollars you can sniff my armpit—one time. Hee hee."

But here we have a lady who isn't a hooker or a Lesbian or an undercover agent, all by herself, looking determined, which she must be all right to keep advancing in the face of Slate, outside admiring his new Coupe De Ville, half a dozen Chicanos with X-ray eyes, and Miss Jungle Fever's two-hundred-decibel, four-minute come.

Slate stopped playing with his electric windows

and caught her by the arm. She bopped his hand with her purse. He grabbed her around the shoulders.

Slate was the best protection a lady could ask for around here, though I doubt it felt like that to her. But instead of screaming or collapsing or whatever ladies in Mercedes cars do in the clutches of six-foot-eight spades in San Jose, she actually smiled—she used the same set of muscles, anyhow—and said, "Could you tell me if a girl named Elizabeth Fenton works here?"

"Elizabeth, Elizabeth?" said Slate, kneading her shoulder; "I can't think of no Elizabeth offhand. We got a Lise without the 'beth' . . . your friend, do she do the act where she put a snake up her cunt?"

The lady sagged. I took pity.

"Let me take her dollar. She can talk to the girls about it."

"She don't have to pay if she just looking. You walk right in, powder puff. I be waiting for when you come back out."

A friendly pat on the oatmeal ass propelled her in the door.

Seeing her coming, the manager rolled his eyes with premonitions of disaster. He'd been having a rough night. About nine-thirty some guy I didn't pay much attention to made a call on the pay phone. A few minutes later I was hitting the Buzzer.

Fat Mary hauled herself to her feet and jogged through the crowd to the bathroom. The manager sent up a new girl from L.A., Charlee, who fielded money the dudes fired up on stage with interesting parts of her anatomy.

Charlee got up there and did a perfectly modest and perpendicular number, but she didn't have a chance. The plainclothesman who blew the whistle over our own pay phone had seen her bouncing quarters off her cunt—probably lobbed a few of his own up there, duly recorded, for evidence, and pointed her out to the cops. Then he stuck a foot out in front of Fat Mary, who was running after a customer who was running out the door with his hand over his face yelling, "Hold on, honey—in this place, you order a beer, you *buy* a beer!" flashed his badge, and told her if she didn't clean up her act next time it would be her turn.

This wasn't any trainee in tennies, either; this was a tan, steel-eyed Senior Vice Squad Narc. Nevertheless, you could hear Mary's answer all over the bar: "Don't you va*gina* me, honey! Don't you come here talking to *me* about touching no vaginas! You ask me, you just as horny and—*ridiculous* as the rest of them. Just cause you got yourself some badge say you entitled to look at cunts—you ought to be *ashamed* of a job like that with all these crooks running around loose and you just hanging out talking about va*gina*s. . . ."

So Fat Mary was hauled off too, leaving Libby, Callie, a beer-seller, and an empty bar. It was just filling up again when this mysterious lady walks in.

Libby was up, starting her second number. One two thump! (jiggle) "I gotta HOT pants."

She had a little trick on this song, she licked her finger and touched her pants, bikini panties with those smile faces all over them, a present from Gerry, as she proudly told everyone, and made a noise like steam, ssssssssss. Hot pants, yeah.

One two thump! (jiggle) ssssssssss "I gotta HOT pants."

"SPREAD THAT HOT LITTLE SLIT FOR US, BABY!"

Sssssssss thump! (jiggle).

The lady was standing just inside the door staring at the stage, looking pole-axed, as they usually do. The manager moved over.

"Who is she?"

"I don't know. She says she's looking for someone who works here, Elizabeth something."

"Elizabeth Taylor, I suppose. Come on—we don't got no goddam Elizabeth. Listen, I think she's Vice. They're out to nail our asses good tonight. And will you look up there. What's this 'sssssssssss' business. Jesus Christ! Tell that kid to keep her hands off her pants. Spread the word. I didn't need this again. Not tonight. Jesus Christ!"

The lady was profiled against the red lights. Her upper lip was drawn back a little over the teeth. This wasn't the Vice, I decided, but it was trouble.

Hot Pants ended and Libby casually lowered the panties with the smiling faces.

One of the regulars, a spade with a strange, strangled voice, called, "How do you like that, fellas? Couldn't you eat the *whoooole* thing?"

"Shee-ut, Ah'll go for anything with a hole in it!" drawled Gerry. Mr. Billy Joe Cool.

Libby made a face at him.

The lady took a deep breath and marched down the bar. She pushed to the front of the crowd. Just before the next song started I heard Libby say "Mother!" Then the jukebox blaring, "Baby, things they are a-changing . . ." kept me from hearing anything else.

Now Libby was standing there pole-axed. She'd picked up her costume and was holding it against her. Her mother was leaning over the bar, waving her hands, pleading silently. "I don't want no nine-to-five routine, rou-tine! . . ." soared the jukebox.

Libby's mother looked around, spotted the steps, and headed right for them.

Libby retreated to the far end of the stage. Her mother emerged from the stairwell.

Gerry jumped up, his hand inside his jacket. Slate marched across the bar. The dudes cheered.

Libby jumped down and ran to the dressing room, stranding her mother up on stage. She was breathing hard and mascara was running down her cheeks, for all the world like a dancer working out.

"TAKE IT OFF, BABY!" somebody yelled.

"TAKE IT OFF!"

"HEY, SHOW US WHAT YOU GOT, MAMA!"

"GIT IT ON, BABY!"

"TAKE IT OFF!"

Libby's mother backed toward the mirror, holding her purse up in front of her. The waves of lust beat up at her. It must have been something to feel.

But she was a mother, endowed with that tiger instinct mothers—most of them, anyhow—seem to have. She regrouped and walked back to the front of the stage.

"Shame on you all!" she yelled. "Do you know how old that little girl is? Do you know how old? She is eighteen years old. *Eighteen years old!* A lot of you are old enough to have a daughter that age. She is only *eighteen* years old."

The men didn't seem as horrified by this announcement as they should have been, but it sure had an effect on the manager. The girls had to be over twenty-one. There was no fun and games with the cops over that. For letting minors in the bar, the ABC could shut Obie's down indefinitely, as well as lay on heavy fines. I remembered with a thud that I was responsible. When Libby first showed up I was in charge after the bust, and in the confusion I never checked I.D.s. And here this dame had to go shouting it three times, in case the boys with the flashlights in their pockets had missed it the first two.

The manager actually hid his eyes against my arm.

But luck was with us. No one jumped up waving a badge.

Gerry leaped up on stage, tie flying, and made to escort the lady down to the floor. She shook his hand off.

"Now hold on a mint, Ma'm—Ah'm Lib-ruh's boy friend."

"*You* are nobody's friend. You are the scum of the earth!" And she marched down off the stage, heading for the dressing room.

The manager stepped in front of her.

"Mother, believe me—we didn't know the girl was underage. It's some kind of mistake. We wouldn't let her work here any more even if she wanted to. But do me a favor. Just let her finish the night, huh? Don't leave me with one dancer and a crowd like this. Could you stick around for a few hours? Tell you what, just to be nice, you stay and it's beers on the house. . . ."

Thus ended Libby's career at Obie's, for the time being anyhow.

She called up on the pay phone half a dozen times a night, asking me what was happening, asking to speak to Gerry, who screamed things like, "Ah miss you too, sugah!" over the sound of the amplifier.

One night she showed up, but the manager wouldn't even let her in the bar, and after an hour necking against cars with Gerry in the parking lot she went home.

So we lost one pair of lovers, but we soon gained another.

A big man at Obie's in those days was our "legal talent." His name was Burton, I think, but the girls called him Button, and soon everyone else did, too. Button was in his early fifties, I'd guess, with silvery hair groomed like something out of an ad. The first time I saw him he was wearing mod boots and a check suit with a belted jacket, the kind of thing they put on male models for the *Playboy* fashion forecast and then forget because nobody buys it. I think **Button must have bought it** in honor of his new clients, because the rest of his outfits were strictly business, gray suits with a silvery tint like his hair, matching tie and handkerchief. Somehow the L.A.-lawyer look evaded his high-rumped figure.

I think Button reminded himself of Greg Bautzer. He reminded me of Winnie the Pooh.

Wherever Obie dug him up, this apparently beat his other responsibilities, and soon he was dropping by several times a week to confer with some girl or other. The girls dug him with his moist, friendly eyes and expensive smell. He was neuter and knowledgeable, like a family doctor, and they rubbed around him and asked his advice: "Hey, Button, my girl friend's old man got busted for transporting, only they didn't have no right to be searching his car, and what she want to know is . . ."

Button, a manicured hand around the bare waist, would lean down to blow impressive terminology into her ear.

"Gee, Pete," he said to me one night, "if I was as young and good-looking as you I'd have a thousand girl friends."

I know there was a Mrs. Button, because she called twice to leave him a message. Her voice sounded thin and chic, and I imagined her sitting in some elegant Santa Clara suburb telling their friends about Burton's *kooky* new cocktail-bar clients, while Burton the Button wallowed in free beer and bottoms in the lowest dive on the Western seaboard.

Button also had extra-legal propensities, as I found one night when I discovered him on his hands and knees in the ladies' room, his wide checkered ass facing the open door. For a moment I thought he'd gone berserk in the bathroom like that other poor slob, but it was, in fact, to prevent anything like that happening again that Button was crawling round and round the toilet.

Button's hobby was electronics, and it was his idea to put an alarm in the bathroom so a girl in the process of being molested could let people know, like one buzz means come quick, two means stay away, I'm digging it.

So here he was in shirtsleeves, his silvery hair sticking out in tufts all over his head, happily running wires around the base of the toilet, over the back, up the sides and over the top of the stall, past the mirror and sink where the wire hung suspended a few inches from the ceiling like a tiny blue-and-white trapeze, and out the door to the bar.

The other end was attached to a large doorbell located right under the toilet paper.

The wires gave the toilet a terrific sinister look, like the Death House at Sing Sing or some kind of mad Pavlovian experiment designed to make people salivate at the sound of flushing.

When it was ready to test, I sat down on the toilet seat, and while Whitey, for authenticity, jammed a knee between my legs, I reached over and rang the doorbell.

Talk about atomic islands! Talk about a thousand smackheads howling in a thousand police ambulances, talk about Vice vans wailing in pursuit of vagrant vaginas—an ululation of exquisite penetration filled the bar.

The half-dozen customers jumped up. The dancer, forewarned, ran off the stage anyhow.

As she charged in the door Button said, "That's good, dear. Come right on over. We'll see how it works with an actual victim. Whitey, run out and give the Buzzer a few squirts. I want to make sure we can tell them apart. Okay, dear, sit right down here and pretend you're about to be raped. All set? Here I am—A COMINA GITCHA!"

The Buzzer produced its monster crow call, BLATT BLATT BLATT; from the depths of the bar responded the Siren, WHEEEEEEEEE! Back and forth they called, sometimes blending in an agony of overtones, sometimes syncopating; BLATT BLATT WHEEEEEEEEE! BLATT WHEEEEEEEEE BLATT WHEEEEEEEEEEBLATTWHEEEEEEE!

The Buzzer had found a mate.

So, presently, did Button.

Lise was the specialest specialty Obie's Los Angeles source ever produced. They'd given us Miss R.H. with her heart-shaped pud; she of the limber labia, Charlee; Renée of Parée; Virgie, who could rotate her boobs in opposite directions and dip her nipples in paint to write her name; and Zahar, the belly dancer, who kept whisky in one of those plastic squeeze lemons and aspirated herself into a stupor every night.

Lise was something else. First of all, she was really foreign, an authentic Hungarian with a deep-voiced accent, unlike Zahar the Egyptian belly dancer from Gilroy, and Renée, whose only accomplishment in her native tongue was "Sex la vive," which, she said, meant, "That's the breaks."

Lise said she was a political refugee, forced to leave after the uprising ("I was only a very young girl, of course"); I couldn't imagine Lise having any concern with politics beyond the Communists shutting down the strip clubs, but I liked to imagine the flight of La Lise, slipping like a serpent through nests of spies, her trunks full of snakes and bangles, iridescent green twining in green sequins.

Lise was also a real snake charmer. Her father, she said, was one of the biggest circus-menagerie directors in Europe, and she moved into the motel with a cage of mice and two boa constrictors named Zoltan and Bela.

Paula came to the bar hysterical: "Petey, I'm popping Vallium like Jujubes just trying to maintain. When I think of what's going on in Twenty-Four—this time Whitey has gone too far. He thinks he can unload any kind of shit on me. Honestly, Petey, there are limits. . . ."

I didn't know which shit provoked the limits: the snakes, the mice, or the fact that Lise also moved in a companion, a girl, whom she addressed with consonant-laden endearments and kissed on the lips in the courtyard, "At ten-thirty in the fucking *morning*," according to Paula.

Finally, Lise was distinguished by the biggest set of knockers anyone at Obie's had ever seen, and counting managers, dancers, and customers, that was an impressive consensus.

She showed them off with no constraint, lifted her blouse, took your hand in a friendly way and encouraged you to touch, as if they were a thing apart from her, exotic pets, like her two snakes, and you were a little shy of reptiles.

Lise was tall, but she didn't look it. She was too earthy, her pull was all downward; I was always surprised when she stood next to me and our eyes were almost level. They were startling eyes, small, close-set, hot-looking, green. Her face was flat and pale and she painted her thin lips white. She wore a platinum wig that enclosed her face like wings.

It wasn't a pretty face or a pretty body—the knockers hung on a flat-rumped, solid frame like those

Michaelangelo women who look like men with two extra hunks of muscle on the chest. Altogether, though, in her long embroidered robes and costumes of fur and snakeskins, with the glittering eyes and deadly pale skin, Lise was a knockout. She managed to make our regulars look like awkward little girls and tired hacks who tasted like old sweat socks to her caviar.

Contrary to Slate's description, Lise did not put a snake up her vagina. It only looked that way. Lise had come prepared to do her regular snake act, but it turned out there was some kind of health law about animals in bars in San Jose. That's all we needed anyhow, an escaped snake or two silently twining through the ooze.

So Lise went out and bought a stuffed toy snake, pink plush with cross-eyes and a bow around its neck. When her turn came to dance, she walked up on stage, spread a large sheepskin redolent of Magyar deserts, and put the pink snake in the middle. Then she went back down and leisurely picked out her music while the men were already cheering and humping their beer mugs.

Lise had a unique walk. She seemed to move as a unit from the hips down, a sort of spoiled-little-girl waddle. For her first number all she did was move around the stage in that sexy waddle, covered from neck to ankles in one of her Cossack robes, circling the sheepskin. When the second song started she knelt down on it facing the audience and took her time opening the top of the robe, inserting the snake through the space of two buttons, slowly exposing those monstrous white breasts, rubbing the snake against them, teasing her nipples with the plush jaws.

105

When the music started again she lay down on her back, perfectly relaxed, a little smile on her thin mouth, opened the robe and raised her legs very slowly, pulled the bottom of her costume up her legs and over her feet, very slowly, and then back down her legs over her belly and breasts, over her mouth and nose, taking a deep breath.

Then she got back up on one elbow and opened her legs. She just lay there, relaxed, with the detached smile, not moving, not simulating anything, just letting it all hang out.

Her cunt was small for such a big girl, very shallow and tight and sparsely haired. The little pink cone stuck out clearly against skin shiny and pale like the petals of an orchid.

And then, for the last song, the snake fixed his cross-eyes on that flower, sniffed deeply the stiff petals and, waving its head back and forth, searched out the source of heavy yellow pollen, dipped into the hidden pistil, and disappeared!

It was awe-inspiring. It went beyond sex. Beer-sellers stood with four poised beers in each hand, watching. All over the bar, glasses were suspended halfway to mouths. The first few times she did it, even the pool game stopped.

It was also an illusion. Actually Lise drew the snake behind her back by the movement of her buttocks, helped along by the hand that was supposedly holding herself open for its penetration. Plush, after all, isn't the texture you need for that kind of thing, plus, I guess, after a while it would get all matted. A real snake, though . . .

The girls tried not to be impressed.

"I don't believe she does it," said Pat.

"At the Orr House," Miss R.H. reminisced over

breakfast, "there was a girl who shoved a banana up for real, and then she just sat there and peeled it and *ate* it."

"Yecccccch!"

"Well, hell, so long as you can peel it. It would be worse if it was something like a cucumber. . . ."

"Yecccccch!"

"You'd have to buy one of those little vegetable-peelers and bring it up on stage with you. . . ."

Button developed the galloping hots for Lise. After a few nights he gave up pretending he was there to talk about his cases. He showed up with flowers. He brought candy. He bought her a filmy baby-doll nighty that she opened in the bar and showed around to everybody.

He stood at the bottom of the steps when she danced, watching every movement, and when she was finished, dressed again in her monklike robe, he held out his hand and she descended regally on his arm.

When Lise's girl friend, an anemic-looking blonde, came to the bar, he stood between them, inclining gallantly. If he was hep to their relationship, which I doubt, he was treating it like just another of Lise's eccentricities; he could share her with a boa constrictor, why not this insignificant creature?

Whitey and I went into the dressing room one night to check something out and surprised Button kneeling in the beer slops in front of a seated Lise. He looked up and chuckled, his Pooh eyes pleading.

"Lise lost one of her earrings," he said.

"It's too bad about that," Whitey said, back in the office. "He'll never get anywhere."

"Because she's a Lesbian?"

"Lise's no Lesbian. She's no queerer than you or

me, except she'll fuck a dude every once in a while if she has to. This is just between you, me, and the fence post—Lise is technically a guy."

"You're shitting me!"

"I know the people in L.A. who handle her. She's one of the guys you read about who have the operations."

"I don't believe it! Jesus, Whitey, what about the boobs?"

Whitey made a plunger out of his thumb and finger and shot some imaginary silicone into my chest.

"I still don't believe it."

"Look, what difference does it make anyhow? I don't care if she's a fucking gorilla that uses Neet. She turns the guys on and they buy more beer—that's all I care."

Callie started coming to work driving what had to be a first for the Obie's parking lot; a silver-gray Jaguar XKL sedan.

I got the usual woolly smile as she walked in.

"Hey, lady, where did you steal that?"

"It's my husband's. Do me a favor, Peter, keep an eye on it. He's so nervous about letting me drive it."

In she went, leaving me wondering why a chick whose husband could afford that kind of Jag needed to work at all, especially in a place like this.

Later that night I got even more curious. It was two-thirty in the morning. We're sitting in the office counting the money when from outside, from the parking lot littered with Ripple bottles, I hear the Chinese waterfalls of a Mozart piano concerto. The sound is so incongruous I think I'm hallucinating again, Mother taking some psychic revenge. But I look outside and there's the Jaguar warming up to a tape of the Twenty-first.

Calliope! What are you doing here with your exotic name and clumsy body, your Victorian fainting spells and your Mozart and your beg pardons?

I didn't give Callie much longer at Obie's. One night she'd be getting ready to leave for work and the thought of it all—the noise, the smell, the X-ray eyes, the evil little girls, and the lonely men, would turn something inside of her. She just wouldn't show up, that night or ever, leaving the manager hysterically short a girl for one night and then nothing, the waves of flesh closing over her passage as if she'd never been.

Instead she kept coming. She showed up at six with her costume in a paper bag and her bottle of juice, got up on stage, sweated, got down, served beer, danced, sweat, beer, sweat, beer beer beer. . . .

With all the running and sweating some good lines started showing through the padding. Her midriff receded, making her breasts stand out more, and you could see her shoulderbones, broad and racy. The halo of hair Fat Mary liberated one night from that spinster bun brought her face into proportion, made it look smaller, more suited to the slender neck. One night her knees made their debut. Another night there were three diamonds of light when she closed her legs.

Her dancing changed, too. This happened with all the girls. At first they worked out on every number, like you do when you're out dancing for fun, but this was eight hours, this was three or four or five nights in a row, and they went around paralyzed the next day, until they learned to cool it, learned the songs they could cruise with, the movements that didn't crucify.

Basic styles didn't change all that much, though. That's one thing I learned for sure at Obie's; the dance is the lady, and the lady is the dance.

Only Callie, it seemed, was nothing in particular, an old burlesque movie that ran down, leaving a blank screen. Then she started turning into the other dancers, one by one.

I doubt anyone noticed but me. The other girls would be too busy hustling, the customers too intent on the vital isoceles. All the managers notice is whether the girl gets up there on time. So I was probably the only one to record this small phenomenon.

She started out with Sandy's little leap. The next night she added the kick and took a classic fall flat on her ass. Her face folded up with pain. The men laughed and clapped.

She started to get up, but then the spirit of Fat Mary took over. Callie dropped back on her stomach and gave a few tight-thighed but willing bumps against the linoleum.

The next night she tried the same thing lying on her back. It was a week before she opened her legs even a millimeter, and even then with a hand stationed between, like a tight end on the line of scrimmage. But pretty soon she was getting it on, flirting with those hungry eyeballs, making them yell:

"TAKE YOUR HAND AWAY WHEN YOU DO THAT, BABY!"

Callie studied the other dancers as closely as the dudes did, two flattening beers forgotten in her hand. She started watching herself in the mirror as she danced, which, due to the state of her eyesight, had her almost on top of it, as if she were trying to dance her way through to the other side.

Her costumes went through changes, too. The old bathing suit gave way to bikini panties, the parachute bra got trimmed with upholstery fringe. She started wearing jewelry; one night a black velvet choker around her neck, the next a dollar diamond ring, once a slave bracelet, a strip of upholstery fringe with jingle bells around her neck, a leather ankle strap, hey! six-inch spike alligator shoes, followed by leopard-skin panties and a flapper-style helmet with a peacock feather sticking out of it. The hair is loose now, welling up around her head like a dandelion fuzzy, which one night twinkles like a thousand jewels under the lights; she's dumped a package of glitter over her head. Now she's got a pair of Woolworth's whory housewife panties with a fly-front zipper which she zips up and down in time to the music: "I'm drowning [zip] drowning in an ocean [zip] of luh [zip zip zip] uv!"

One night I came to work with the autobiography of the Hungarian violinist Szigeti, which, probably influenced by the arrival of Lise, I'd taken out my last time at the library. Callie noticed it as she walked in.

"Peter," she said, "you know how to *read!*"

This was not an altogether frivolous comment. The bosses had recently gotten very paranoid about the Vice, and the bar was covered with notices about "lude activities and costumze" which the girls laboriously read, tracing down the lines with their fingers, lips moving.

But when she picked it up, her eyes widened for real. She gave me another one of those hard looks.

"I used to play," I yelled.

"Who did you study with?"

"Cat named Matteo."

"*Raymond* Matteo?"

Now my eyebrows went up. What does a bottomless dancer in San Jose know about violin teachers? I was bragging a little about Matteo, of course. I'd only been with him for four months, though it was a very intensive thing, a summer workshop he was giving on the West Coast that I got into by a lucky fluke.

My real teacher was Mr. Greenberg, an elderly German who always seemed to wear the same blue-wool suit winter and summer and wouldn't touch his violin before he'd dipped his fingers in warm orange juice. It had to be fresh-squeezed orange juice, too, not canned or frozen, and one of the rituals of my young life was Mother rotating oranges on a glass juicer while I sat at the kitchen table, my baby nuts shrinking back up into my body in anticipation of his arrival. I still have the scar on my elbow where Mother whammed me with the violin bow for eating all the oranges in the house the morning of my lesson.

Szigeti comes across from his memoirs as a pretty worldly cat—he was, after all, Hungarian. Matteo was a pretty raunchy guy, too. One day he told us how hard it was not to sleep with his wife while he practiced for a performance, which is what gave me, at age seventeen determined to get laid without delay or jump off the Golden Gate, the idea that led to Sandra Matteo.

Mr. Greenberg, though. The incongruity of sitting at Obie's thinking about Mr. Greenberg floored me—Mr. Greenberg who had spent twelve years training my ears toward the most infinitesimal differentiations in intonation, while here I was having my hearing destroyed by endless shattering repetitions of the same blatant four-note melodies.

Why, for eight years I never knew he had a *first* name. I took it for granted that when he popped out of his mother, wearing a tiny impeccable dark-blue pin-stripe suit, she said, "I will name him Mr. Greenberg."

Then my own mother, in one of her letters, said, "How is Friedpert? Do you 'ever' see your 'old' teacher?"

Friedpert! And what's this with the quotation marks! Come to think of it, Mother's epistolary style, bristling with exclamation points and quotation marks, is a lot like Obie's.

No, "Mother," I never did see my old teacher. From the age of seven to the age of nineteen we had our weekly sessions of orange juice and "Ve re*peat*, yah?"; in some ways Mr. Greenberg had more of an impact on my character than my father, bumping vaguely around the house in his floppy pajamas or tootling away down by the furnace. But after I stopped my lessons Mr. Greenberg just disappeared.

Sitting here under the amplifier I suddenly flash. My mother and Mr. Greenberg. All those hours she locked me in my room to practice—the way I had copies of *Boys' Adventures* hidden between the covers of my Blumenstengel Scale Studies, so she had Mr. Greenberg. First he had to dip his pecker in warm, freshly squeezed orange juice. No wonder Mother got so upset that day I ate all the oranges. They were probably together right now in some southern eternity of oranges.

Stern, you are going mad! He was at least sixty the first day you ever set eyes on him.

"Callie," I yelled. "Who the hell are you?"

But she had gone already to change into her costume.

I asked her again later that night, screaming through the lattice while she was rolling around on the floor of the stage. She yelled back, "Have you ever heard of the Mandelbaum Music Scholarship? That's my grandmother."

While I'm digesting this—the Mandelbaums are one of San Francisco's old money-and-culture families, always in the paper for sponsoring this and that artistic event, and at the time I still thought of going to a music college I was actually a runner-up in that competition—Callie pops up by the door with two beers for some dudes who just walked in. Their eyes zero in on her crotch, and already they're having a hard time getting their hands in their pockets for change.

"I used to play too," she yelled. "My grandmother had a crush on Galamian, so they started me on the cello. But every time I had to play for someone or audition or anything I'd faint. Just like I did here. It happens whenever I'm really nervous. My husband even tried to hypnotize me out of it—he's a doctor—but it didn't work. I've put off my Ph.D. orals for seven years because I know what will happen as soon as I walk in the door."

Doctor husband. Right. Ph.D. Right.

"Callie—what are you doing here?"

"Peter—what are you?"

And, smiling, she took a quarter tip for the two beers.

One night somebody started a fire in the ladies' room. Smoke might have been oozing round the door for hours without being noticed in the general smokey stench; the first anyone knew was, a girl who had gone in to use the toilet ran out shrieking. A general milling ensued at the back of the bar, but the dudes with their eyes welded to the stage remained oblivious until the dancer herself saw the smoke, screamed, and ran out into the parking lot, stark nekkid. Gerry and Slate tried to get into the bathroom, but the smoke was too thick. Suddenly the Siren, shorted by the heat, started its Mach Three mooing: WHOOEEEEEEEEEEE! Panic!

Everyone headed for the door at once. A few oldsters tottered along the bar, trying not to get crushed. WHOOOEEEEEEE! WHOEEEEEEEEEEEE!

The manager, hanging desperately on to the pay phone as the crowd made away with his lower half, yelled, "Where the hell are they when you need them? Leave one lousy faucet out of the sprinkler system and the Fire Marshal's all over your ass in five minutes. You get a ten-alarm blaze and it takes them three hours to get the dog in the truck." WHOOOEEEEEEEEE! WHOOOEEEEEEEEEE!

Atomic island! Twenty-five seconds before the toilet bowl reached Critical Mass. WHOOOEEEEEEE! WHOOOEEEEEEEEE!

From under a cloud of greasy black smoke comes a "whoop" as a pool player makes the eight ball.

And here they come, red light flashing, siren wailing, five firemen in full gear, with their axes held at the ready and twenty-five miles of Zoltan-like hose.

All this, and what they find in there is a pile of greasy rags.

The Siren resisted all attempts to stifle it. Finally they had to cut the wires, which was the end of the Siren, because once something breaks at Obie's it stays broken unless it's absolutely vital to the pushing of beer.

The fire left long black blistery streaks in the whorehouse-orange paint, and rather than go to the trouble of repainting the whole bathroom they stuck a red bulb in the socket, which obscured the damage, even gave it a rather decorative effect, but which, Callie told me, she could not help feeling created the atmosphere of a miniature red-light district.

I had asked Callie out to breakfast three nights in a row. Her regrets sounded plausible. The four-year-old was up at seven, which meant she was getting by on four hours sleep a night even if she drove straight home, maybe a nap during the day when Luke took his, then starting at five o'clock the grueling eight hours again.

True, she had deep circles under her eyes, and when the pressure was off she moved like a deep-sea diver.

117

The third time she turned me down I decided fuck it and finished the night with ten beers, buying only from Callie and elaborately tipping her the quarter each time. Then I asked a pretty Chicana named Annie, who ate silently and ravenously and made no bones about coming to my room after her sausage and eggs.

About six in the morning she shook her reeking hair off my face and said she had to get going. The next time I saw her she was finishing the dayshift, up on stage flashing the breasts and/or genitalia I had recently messed up.

She woke me up at the motel the next day around noon and we fucked some more.

That night she didn't show up. The agency must have sent her somewhere else.

Adios one member of *la raza*, hello to another.

Snowy Ayala was a deejay on KLAR, San Jose's Spanish-language station. Obie hired him to plug the bar on his program. Snowy dropped down one night to see what the scene was all about and dug it so much he offered to M.C. a show or two just for fun and free beer.

One Friday night he came with his own mike and amplifier and set up next to the jukebox. He sat on a barstool rapping into the mike and rocking back and forth like Ray Charles, a little brown dude with pointed eyeteeth and wraparound shades. He spoke fast, unaccented English, interspersed with machine-gun cadenzas of Spanish. The microphone made unbearable feedback noises; the Chicanos all yelled and banged their glasses on the tables whenever he went into Spanish, adding just so many more ergs of noise and confusion to the existing bedlam.

We had our usual Friday-night visit from the cops, heralded by a Stern obligato on the Buzzer, and Snowy rapped hysterically through the whole thing. As the dancer galloped toward the ladies' room: "Look at that girl go! Look at her go! If this was Bay Meadows I'd lay a fiver on that little filly. What's that? You'd like to lay something on her yourself? Hut! Hey, look at that dude running out the door. Hold on a second, *charro*, if you leave me your name and address I'll mention you to the Olympic Track Committee. Hut! I don't think I dig the way you folks welcome the cops. You know what that alarm sounds like? Everyone zipping up their flies into a microphone all at once. I think it would look better if you had a guy outside blowing a trumpet like they do in the Robin Hood movies. Hey, look what's here. Doo-too-too-too-too-da-dooooooo! Good evening to you, Officer. Why don't you step right up and introduce yourself. He seems to be a little shy. I don't blame him. A sensitive guy like him could get a rotten shock coming into this place. Hut! *Puerco! Cabron! Apuesto que no sabes quien es tu padre!*"

The rest of the night he introduced the dancers and provided a scurrilous running commentary that displayed considerably more energy than the dancing.

"Coming up now we have—what's your name again sweetheart? Denise! Little Denise, and she'll be giving us her interpretation of—oh goody, for only the three hundredth time tonight it's . . . "Jungle Fe-vah!" Do it to it, Denise. Denise is our youngest dancer, she's only twelve years old. Excuse me, Denise, that's not true, gang, she's actually an extremely young-looking eighty. They kicked her out of the old-age home because she was driving all the old-timers wild chasing her around in their wheel chairs. I see one of them followed her right here to the bar. Watch it, Gramps, if you don't close your mouth I'm afraid your teeth are gonna fall right into your beer. Maybe he thinks it's a glass of Efferdent. Kind of tastes like it, doesn't it? Except this beer cleans the slime off your teeth a lot faster. No, folks, Denise knows I'm only kidding, she's a great dancer and a great sport. I talked to her a little while ago, and she tells me her real ambition is to be a beautician. I think she had a great career ahead of her—she just curled my hair without even coming near me. Hut!"

"Peter, for goodness sake!" said Callie, "don't tell him anything about me if he asks."

"Why not?"

"Because it's irrelevant who I am or what I do outside these walls. I'm a dancer, and I sell beer, that's all. I'm just a dancer."

Snowy did ask me about her, and I told him a few things anyhow. Her next time up he said, "O.K., gang, while you're still quivering over lovely little Lola, here comes proof that good things come in big packages too—Candy! Kelly? Collie! You're put together a lot better than Lassie, sweetheart. *Mamasoto!* Collie is a bit of a mystery woman, folks. I asked her about herself and she said her lips are sealed. Of her *mouth*, dummy. But funny you should mention it, I do happen to know that Collie had a little accident on the way to the bar tonight. She had a tube of Epoxy in her pocket in case her G-string broke and the tube broke open right there in her pants. That's why her thighs are stuck together like that. Watch it in the front row there, if she ever opens her legs you'll all get high on the fumes. *Glue* fumes, wise guy—what a bunch of dirty minds in here tonight. No, seriously, *amigos,* Collie has a friend in the bar who revealed to me something that the lady was too modest to tell me herself."

"Peter!" yelled Callie.

"It seems she is down here at Obie's incognito —dig that word—hut! Because up in San Francisco . . ."

"How *could* you!" yelled Callie.

". . . is none other than the world-famous stripper, THUNDER LA BOOM!"

"Is he crazy?" yelled Callie.

". . . got tired of being mobbed by her fans wherever she goes. She just wants to take her clothes off in peace. That's all of us want, isn't it? A little piece? You'll excuse me if I seem to be having trouble with my articulation. When she does that my tongue sticks to the roof of my mouth. Articulation, right? That's what we're all doing underneath our coats. Hut! Go for it, Thunder baby. Do it to it, Thunder!"

"Peter!"

"It could have been worse," I yelled. "I could have told him you were Lightning La Crash."

Then Callie blew my mind by asking *me* out to breakfast.

"What's the matter," I said lightly. "Have a fight with the old man?"

I didn't expect a serious answer, but she sighed and lowered her head. "No. We don't even do that any more."

Shit! Don't tell me she asked me out just to sound off about her marriage. I wasn't going for any more of these in-and-out sagas.

But Callie dropped it herself, as if even the little she'd said embarrassed her, and we talked about music, about her work for the degree—for the last seven years she'd been happily writing a thesis on one of the world's three great pessimists.

But no matter what we talked about, the conversation kept coming back to Obie's.

"Let's not talk about the bar," we both said several times.

"You know, Peter," she finally said, "I think what it comes down to is I can't help talking about the bar. I'm obsessed. Would you believe Libby and I used to talk about it nonstop all the way to work and all the way back, every night—otherwise the thing kind of haunts you. You have these dreams all night long and all day. Then people ask me what it's like to be a bottomless dancer, and I can't tell them. I don't think anyone who hasn't been in that place night after night and week after week could possibly understand. I once tried to tell my husband. It's hopeless."

"Try me," I said, right on cue.

So she told me. Boy, did she tell me. Before she was finished the sun was coming up and Leroy was stacking the chairs on the tables.

Okay, she'll begin at the beginning. She's supposed to be at Obie's ready to go at six o'clock, but for her the whole thing starts hours earlier. Around three a little clutch in the stomach. After that it's no use trying to concentrate on anything. The feeling is hard to describe: half dread, half excitement. She gets washed—face, underarms, between her legs.

"I beg your pardon, Peter, but you're going to get the straight dope, in all its gory details. I—well—I *drip* a lot. I always have. Am I digusting you?"

She thinks about that a lot when she's up there dancing.

"One time I heard a man say to his friend, 'She's wet.' Just like that, very matter-of-fact. 'She's wet.' I don't know why that got to me so bad. Maybe the tone of voice, like I was a mare and some guy was sticking his fist up me to see if I was ready for the stallion. He's say it in the same way. 'She's wet, boys. Bring him over.' "

Now she uses a Tampax all the time, which an incident she'd rather not even talk about taught her to cut the string off first. She was worried about something showing even so and checked it out in a mirror.

"Oh, Peter, I've been married for twelve years and I have two children, and I'd never seen myself down there. That's how shy I've always been. After a month and a half at Obie's, here I am talking to a stranger about my drips."

Well, after the drip patrol she puts on her make-up. Callie never used make-up, for one reason or another. When she first started at Obie's she went berserk for a while there, setting Luky loose in Woolworth's toy department so she could prowl around the make-up counter, days on end, weighing Smoky Emerald against Apricot Beige, Sugar Plum Frostee, Honey Rum Parfait. You can blush, lash, gloss, whip and slick yourself a thousand different ways at Woolworth's.

Not to speak of things for the hair: "Peter, when I was a kid my mother used to pull my hair back so tight people thought I was Chinese."

Before she was allowed anywhere near water, her head was swathed like a swami, first a net, then a towel, then a mob cap, all topped by a giant plastic shower cap, a rig designed to keep her suppressed curls from springing back, under the influence of moisture, like a thousand tiny mousetraps, or in the language of the jars of hair-straighteners they kept trying on her, "reverting."

Reverting. Right there on the bathmat. Under the hydrocephalic turban. Frankenstein clutching his hem-stitched neck. . . .

"When I came to Obie's I understood for the first time what my mother and grandmother were fighting. One night I walked out there and I was surrounded by naturals as far as the eye could see, and I said to myself, 'Callie, they may have told you your hair looks like Brillo, but what they meant was kinks. Your hair has *soul*. Right, on hair.' "

For weeks on end she prowled around bargain shops, too, the phantom of the Goodwill, ogling the gold shoes with the six-inch spikes and the feather boas, feeling like Clark Kent among the corset-tossing housewives: beneath this mild-mannered exterior is the queen of the strippers, Thunder La Boom. Yes! Thunder!

"I think somewhere inside me there's always been someone who jumped out of cakes. I know Obie's is low and vile, and nobody really gives a damn, but somewhere in back of it all there's a Platonic honky-tonk with chandeliers and ladies in feathers who are very wise and warm in the ways of men. That's where Thunder works, dancing on the bar. I try to be in that place when I'm working too."

Callie's ready to leave the house by quarter to five. That's leaving a lot of time, but she drives slow. She hugs the kids, but they can't kiss her because of the make-up.

Dancing mother stays in the slow lane doing forty, so anxious about the drive that there's no room to be anxious about what's at the end of it. Traffic on 280 is always bumper-to-bumper, though, and she has time to start feeling those little blips of anxiety, like radar scanning, that started at three and come closer and closer, until by the time she turns off the freeway there's a constant static in her stomach. How to describe this voluptuous feeling of humiliation? Maybe like once when she was a kid reading a report in front of the class, and suddenly she had to pee real bad. Helplessness, excitement, fear, and deep, deep reluctance.

As soon as she pulls into the parking lot she's caught in the trip, automatically noting the number of cars, judging how many customers, how many tips to start her night off. If she's lucky, Slate, who considers pawing the girls a privilege of his position and is just too damn big for anyone to convince him otherwise, won't be hanging around outside, waiting to get first grabs at the girls as they come in. And here I am, Peter, sitting on my stool by the door, long legs propped on the table, a T-shirt and faded jeans and scuffy hair, looking incongruous and cheering under the flashing lights.

The sound of the music as she walks across the lot brings another surge of that ambiguous emotion. The minute she's inside the door there's no more ambiguity. She breathes in the smell and hates to be here, hates the men who turn to look at the fresh meat, hates the sweating girl up on stage cranking out her last set of the day, hates the dressing room, hates the smell of stale beer. Why should stale beer smell so bad?

Callie is sitting on a keg in her costume, surrounded by notices, putting on her shoes. To make things worse, another night girl comes in, and it's Pat. Callie is afraid of Pat; physically afraid. The night before Pat pushed Callie out of her way so hard she fell into the sink.

But Pat's in a good mood tonight.

"You on the rag or something?" she bellows in greeting. "I got something *good* for the cramps."

She holds out a bottle of something called Cream of Kentucky.

"Peter, I'm not a drinker. I don't drink, I don't smoke, I don't use drugs. One of my first nights at Obie's, Delise asked me if I had any beans, and

I asked her if she meant baked beans or jumping beans. I know what they all think of me around here, and they're right. I'm a drip. But I took a big swallow of that whisky. I guess I was afraid she'd hit me over the head with the bottle if I turned her down."

Callie blasts out of the dessing room, on top of things again, feeling her six miles of legs in the six-inch spikes, the chain she wears around her hips jingling, all the guys looking at her. Thunder!

She walks into the office to get her bank. The dayshift girls are coming in to check out. Day girls are the bottom of the barrel even by Obie's standards. One creature in a wig of blond sausage curls has got to be close to sixty, flushed from a honorable senescence by some family calamity. Callie envies them all anyhow, because they're done. They can get dressed and walk out with a waiting old man, home to dinner.

Callie gets to have dinner twice a week, on her days off. And she walks out alone.

She gets her bank with the pink card in it: her name, tap, starting figure for the tap, amount of bank. Here she is, Colleen (this Joe must be Irish), "A" tap, 6297, $25 bank.

Callie is happy. "A" is a good tap, right next to the glasses cooler, the tap closest to the stairs and on the top bank of taps so she won't have to bend so much. "A" drawer is also one of the top drawers in the register.

She goes out, puts her bank away, and draws a beer to see how "A" is pouring tonight. She's learning the fine art of catching spills. The managers all swear they'll fire a girl on the spot if they catch her even thinking about it, but it's all right if you're careful. A good juicy tap yields an extra glass every three or four. A normal tap takes six or more pours to make one spill. Catching spills adds a little spice to the evening, outfoxing the manager, and every so often that automatic seventy-five cents in the tip compartment.

"A" is juicy tonight. Hooray! She takes the beer and walks out to sell it. She feels a bit special about the first beer she sells every night. If she gets to keep the quarter, it will be a good night for tips. Here comes the lucky gentleman: balding, hornrims, car coat, in he comes with a rush and keeps going. Like a lot of men who don't usually come to a place like this, he's covering his uneasiness with impetus. He doesn't know where you're supposed to sit, or what you're supposed to do, and in his heart he expects to find a committee composed of his mother, wife, children, boss, and a superior-court judge with a warrant, so as soon as he's in he keeps moving, fast. The girl with the beer is the lifesaver; something to do with hands: take beer, reach for wallet, can't get it out with one hand, chuckle chuckle. Contact Acceptance.

Comes the moment of revelation. Callie holds out the tip tray, practicing E.S.P. on him: You do not want this quarter, you do not want this quarter, you do not want . . .

He reaches for the quarter. She moves the tray away. You do not want this quarter, you stingy rat crum. . . . He picks it up, realizes it's the only change on the tray, dismisses it with a backward flick of the fingers, already engrossed in the dancer's cunt.

"Thank you *very* much. Thank you!"

He didn't want the quarter! And she's truly, heartbreakingly grateful. He has started her evening off well, poor jerk, in his sporty coat. After all, none of this is his fault.

Happy, Callie puts the quarter in the left-hand compartment of her drawer, the one she uses for tips. The third dancer comes out of the dressing room. It's Donna, an agency girl who doesn't put much energy into the job. Better and better. There are some dancers it's very hard to follow, like Lise or Fat Mary, but Pat and Donna are a good contrast to her own style.

Callie is suddenly elated. She claps as Pat finishes a dance, yells, "Come on, fellas, show some appreciation."

She loves to collect words like fellas, gents, mister, boys, stud; Thunder words. Thunder is, of course, also a notorious curser. Why, as the fellas used to say in the old saloon where Thunder got her start, that gal can out-cuss a Texas mule-driver. But the words stick in Callie's throat.

"I mean I can say 'fuck.' There. 'Fuck.' But I can't *really* say it. It doesn't well from the depths at moments of emotion. I've been practicing. I stand behind the bar and say 'fuck' in time to the music."

But the fellas don't respond to Callie's exhortation.

"That's right—get your hands out of your pockets," bellows Pat from the stage, which gets laughs and a few claps. Callie still has a lot to learn. "Appreciation" is no good—about four syllables too long and too abstract, with undertones of nagging spouses.

She washes some mugs. She has turned this into an exercise, five mugs in each hand, lifted high from sink-to-sink: I MUST (slosh) I MUST (slosh) I MUST INCREASE MY BUST (slosh).

She sells four more beers, fifty cents tips and seventy-five for a spill in the tip compartment, then she's up.

Callie punches her music. Although the jukebox

tends to come up with the songs in some cranky order of its own, Callie tries to gear the song to the state of undress. The first dance, in costume, needs to be lively, because there're no private parts in view to distract. The second song needs a steady beat to go with the strut she's developed that takes little effort and keeps her liberated boobs bobbing.

"WOW, JUST LIKE A BOWL OF JELLO!" someone yells; "SOFT-BOILED EGGS!" yells another.

The third song her pants are off, and she can coast on her merits, so to speak. The fourth song something slow and sweet, and she goes down, down.

It's funny about the first set of the night. Sometimes the guys really get off on her, fresh and clean and full of positive energy. Sometimes she draws a blank, she's not warmed up, still oriented to the outside world and the dying strip of day she can see with a pang past my profile out the door.

It's like that tonight. The jukebox sabotages her from the start by playing the slow song first, and rolling around on the floor in her costume misses the whole point of the exercise, which is a rest after the first three with the nakedness to carry it off. That also means she'll have to work out on the fourth song when she's really tired, plus take the chain off right away, because she can't go down with the chain on, it cuts into her, which means another workout on the third song without the chain to distract. . . .

Such are the calculations that occupy her mind all night long, that mind which until recently wandered with her pessimist through such topics as the existence of God and whether Nature is good or evil; now it applies itself to such questions as, given the presence of a rapist in the bathroom and the police right outside the door, does one run into the ladies' room to avoid the police and get attacked, or does one stay up there to avoid getting attacked and get arrested?

"No, really, I'm serious. They're beginning to worry about me at home. Every time the phone rings I run into the bathroom."

It's the fourth song. Nobody claps, and Callie is depressed again. Her make-up job is beginning its long agony, the adrenalin is all played out, she's dirty and hot and *that is it,* eight hours of it, fifteen, twenty more times up there with the eyes on her, the tongues flicking, the tight grins.

Back into her costume and down the three steps, the change of levels, from stage to floor, from the Untouchable to Target. The eyes still swollen with her nakedness swarm on her. She races behind the bar. Tonight, unfortunately, one of a party of salesmen on his way out decides to get the last drop out of his dollar, and Callie, hurrying hot and depressed to the sanctuary of the taps, has the shock of a sudden grab between her legs.

The bar clock says six-forty-five.

People start coming in.

"Would you care for a beer, sir?"

"Yeah, gimme one. You want a beer, Jack?"

"Sure, I'll take one. Thanks, honey."

"Seventy-five cents? What kind of a place is this? I just paid a dollar to get in."

"Keep the change, sweetheart."

"Do you dance? When's your turn?"

"What's your name?"

"Bring us five more, sweetheart. Say, come here first. Come here. I won't bite. Ron says *he'll* bite. Shut up, Ron. What's your name? Let me introduce you to my friend. Thunder, this is Ron. Ron, this is Thunder. Ron's a little shy. Look at Ron, he's cracking up, he don't believe it. Yeah, we all work at the same place. Try to guess. Ever hear of Nucraft? That's us. Nucraft carpets. We sell carpets because we like to lay things, ahahahahahahah! Somebody slap Ron on the back, he's choking to death."

Concentrate, Callie. She's got a five-dollar bill to cover the five beers, two dollar bills for two singles, another two for two beers together, four quarters, one of which is a tip. . . .

Callie has trouble remembering who gets what change, she tries to pick out a quick characteristic to help her remember, some clothing, feature, impression: twenty-five cents Slimy Oriental; fifty cents Weasel Nose, thank you, sir; Purple Tie Acne, Cowboy Hat, but who is this extra quarter?

"Hey, where's my change!" yells Polka-Dot Teeth.

May your life be full of cavities, you rotten . . . Callie! Over a lousy quarter wishing such dental rot on this poor rodent. How evil I'm getting. I shouldn't care about the damn quarter.

But she does. Passionately. The minute she gets out of Obie's a quarter is just a quarter again, but in here it's a token, a talisman, ammunition in a battle of will powers, a counter in a game her ego has to win.

The funny thing is, she's never paid attention to money; it's always been there, and she's always been careless about it. In fact, that's part of the reason she's here in the first place. One of her husband's favorite lines: "If you'd ever in your life had to go out and *earn* some of the goddam stuff . . ." and suddenly one time she started thinking about it.

There were a lot of things she'd never done. She'd never lived by herself, worked, filled out a tax form, opened a bank account, driven a car.

"It would have been so easy for me, Peter, just switch onto automatic pilot and end up like my mother, totally dependent on a strong man. But the more I thought about it the more I realized I was stifled, and whatever I'd had with my husband was stifling along with me. Here I was going on thirty-five, and not once in my life had I stood on my own two feet. I've got my mother and my grandmother, either of whom would gladly support me for the rest of my life. My husband—he'd give me money without asking anything. He's a good man. He'd be glad to let me do my own thing. It may seem insane to you for me to be doing all this with so much money in the background. But I've got to do it on my own. I'm saving every penny I make, I'll get a little car and be ready to take my kids and set up somewhere. I hope it doesn't come to that. I hope I can become my own person without tearing my home up. We're together in our hearts, goodness knows, it's just everything else that's a mess."

Never mind, as soon as she had her big revelation she enrolled in driving school and sent letters to every college in the Bay Area offering herself as the world expert on obscure Romantic pessimists. Only one of them even bothered to answer.

"After a month of want ads where does Miss Financial Disaster of the Year end up? As a teller at the Bank of America. It was the best I could do. At the end of my first week I was a hundred dollars short. The manager agreed to forget it if I gave up my plans for a banking career. Then I got a job packing Brussels sprouts in a frozen-food plant. One day a girl fainted, someone beside me for a change, and her hand got caught in the packaging machine. When

I saw her hand *I* fainted. I'd just started a job as breakfast cook at an old-age home when Libby—she was baby-sitting for me—decided to become a go-go dancer, and I tell you that old-age home was so depressing I took my middle-aged spread and my Mommy boobs in my hand and tagged along. It was the bravest thing I ever did in my life."

The bar clock reads seven-fifty, and she's got a five and three ones and some quarters in her tips. Very good, sure to top thirty if it keeps up like this. She always keeps the corner of her eye open on the door. She sees me straighten up on my stool, which means customers, and pours a couple—oh damn! there's about thirty seconds left on Donna's last song.

Run like hell: "Care for a beer, sir?" The question is a formality. She's standing there dripping foam on their shoes.

"Sure, when we get a seat."

"I don't think you'll find one right now. Why don't you take the beer and I'll keep my eyes open . . ."

Buy, dammit! Donna's putting her pants back on. Oh, no, a twenty-dollar bill!

"O.K., who's next!" The manager, obscene little man, clapping importantly.

". . . seventeen, eighteen, nineteen, and twenty . . ." (You do not want those two quarters, you do not . . .)

NEXT!

A9, G7, R0, B2.

Sometimes she actually feels like an entertainer instead of a martyr. She extends herself, gets off on the applause and the hoots. All right. Thunder is *up*.

"Oh, Peter, you must understand I've been a big, awkward, timid creature all my life. I know that a female elephant would get a hand up there if she'd bend over, but damn it, it's still good for the old ego. Do you know how many propositions I get a night? *Me?*"

"Hey, baby, can I ask you a question? Do you . . . supplement your income?"

"Do you—eh—date the customers?"

"How much do you want for thirty minutes?"

"I got forty dollars. What time you get off?"

"Forget it mister," says Thunder. "The only thing I sell is beer." Hut!

"Say, can I ask you something? How much would it cost me to rent you for ten minutes?"

"*Rent* me! That's an odd way of putting it. Makes me feel like a U-Haul."

"I said exactly what I meant. I want to rent you for ten minutes, right here, just to sit down and talk to me. Five dollars?"

"In the first place I couldn't just sit down for ten minutes. I've got a job to do. In the second place, you can't *rent* people's attention. It's ridiculous."

"Is that so? What if I offered you twenty dollars. Thirty dollars! Hah! For five minutes. What would you say then?"

"Now I am getting offended. I tell you what, I'll go back and bring you a beer, and we'll forget you ever tried to rent me. Just say 'Hey sweetheart, can I talk to you for a few minutes,' and see what happens . . ."

"Would you like a beer, sir?"

"I still got some. Hey, baby, are you married?"

"Yes, I am."

"That's too bad."

"No it isn't!"

"Lemme tell you something. If I was married to a broad like you she wouldn't be working in no topless joint. What's your old man think of this?"

Yes, what does he think? Well, he's being liberal about it—he can hardly tell her she's too dependent and then object to a job where she makes almost as much as he does. But then he really doesn't know what he's being liberal about. Instinctively the way she describes the place is more Platonic honky-tonk than Obie's. Of course, it cuts into their—lives—a great deal. When she gets home at three in the morning she just flops down on the couch—it's easier than taking a shower—so she won't stink the bed up, probably rousing Luke, who's a light sleeper and wakes like a puppy, instantly alert and ready to play. Well, to be perfectly honest, Obie's manages to turn her off completely. That's the way she feels these days. She feels that men all want the same thing from her, it doesn't matter if they're husbands or friends or the police or the eighty-year-old man at the drug store. All they want is to see her vagina.

She's meat. To men, she's meat.

(Small pause, while Stern contemplates the talkative hamburger sitting across from him.)

Cowboy, Greasy Sideburns, Spade/Beanie; you do not want this quarter, you do not want this . . .

"Hey, you were real good, honey. I liked your act."

"Are you married?"

"If you ever got termite problems, look me up. Here's my card. That's me on the bottom, Sam the Termite Man."

"What's your name?"

"What are you doing after work?"

"Give me twenty minutes, sweetheart . . . I'll have you moaning."

"Can I buy you breakfast?"

"Could you do me a favor? Could you . . . brush against me accidentally when you pass by?"

"What's your name?"

"Can I ask you a question? Would you mind if I touched you? Just on the arm. I want to feel the warmth. You're the first woman I've seen like this in three years. I just got out of Soledad this morning."

Before her own arrest, Callie would have received this information with righteous horror. Now she feels filled with solidarity.

"What they send you up for?" says Thunder out of the side of her mouth. One night may not be the same as three years, but it gives you an idea, and she gives him a whole hug.

"Are you married?"

Is Thunder married? Do cows moo? Thunder has had more husbands than tits on a sow, as they say back in the old saloon. But ever ready to march with the times, she signs herself Ms. La Boom—Thunder to you, handsome.

"Got one for you, sweetheart. What word has four letters, ends in -unt, and is totally feminine?"

"Don't tell me. I want to think about it. I'll be back."

Red Sweater, Spastic, Basketball Head (you do not want this quarter), I must-slosh-I must—slosh —hunt? Women hunt for men. Runt? Geezer, Dwarf, Oriental/Cowboy (you do not, slosh, I must . . .), Bunt? Grunt? Punt?

"Give up? It's *aunt!* Haw haw haw!"

"Oh, but that's marvelous! That's really good."

"All right, here's another for you. Pay attention. Why are seven bottomless dancers lined up, first one with her face to the wall, the second with her ass to the wall, then face, ass, face, face face, like the Lone Ranger?"

The bar clock says—oh, no, it can't be, only eight-thirty! She's been here two and a half hours, five and a half to go, she'll never make it. Despair.

Callie heads for the dubious haven of the door marked OMEN—somebody recently rubbed out the w and will probably soon go to work on the o, which should liven things up at the back of the bar.

With the shredded wires hanging off the toilet and with the red light, it's distinctly weird in there, but she enjoys the peace of just sitting for a minute unmolested. It's a mistake to stop moving at Obie's, though. Suddenly she is attacked by a Moment of Truth: *Quo vadis*, Calliope Zipser? You are thirty-four years old, you have two children, a respectable husband, a Master's Degree in Romantic Pessimism, and your grandmother was once on intimate terms with Mischa Elman. What are you doing sitting here in a G-string emasculating Tampax while you try to figure out why seven bottomless dancers are like the Lone Ranger?

And from outside Joe Simon sings the answer, wailing to the world that no matter what it is, you gotta do your thang.

"I am doing—my—thang," says Callie to herself. "Whatever that may be. I'm sure I'll find out sooner or later."

Callie runs out of the bathroom and up on stage, thinking maybe this job is O.K. in a gruesome kind of way. But there're two guys sitting by the steps, and they've been ordering Cokes they top off out of a bottle.

"Hey, it's the big one," yells one of them in a

"she's wet" tone of voice, and his friend gives a few drunken hoots; Greasy and Slimy, as Callie promptly names them, are evidently going to put on their own entertainment.

Callie does some of her difficult stuff right away, trying to keep her audience.

"That's *right*, baby," yells Greasy. "Limber them muscles up real good so you can spread nice and pretty for us."

"Yeah!" yells Slimy, the back-up man.

Callie does her lead-in to the second dance. She doesn't just take her top off while she's waiting for the music. She's borrowed the tease principle from Miss R.H., and she takes it off slowly while she's dancing.

"Quit fooling around, sweetheart!" yells Greasy. "We don't need no ballet. Just show us what you got! Get your boobs out here!"

"Yeah, boobs! Let's see the boobs!"

At this point Callie stubs her toe in that little rip in the linoleum the cheap bastards *never* fix no matter how many times the girls tell them, just like they'll never clean up the dressing room or paint the bathroom, just like the pay checks will always be a little short, and they make you dance with the blood dripping out of you onto the stage—the sense of exploitation hits her like a pain, and the bottom falls out again. She's sick, disgusted; she wants to go *home*.

Taking off her top she feels like she's loosing Christians to the lions. Forgive me, gallant Super-bosom!

"Now you're talking! Shake them jellies. Hey!"—turning to Slimy—"You like boobs? You like to suck on boobs?"

"You better believe I like to suck on boobs!"

"You like to suck on one of those boobs right now?"

"Oh, yeah, oh, yeah! Suck!"

"I tell you, I sure could dig one of them nipples in my mouth now. I'd eat the whooooole thing!"

Emboldened by laughs, Greasy moves up a step and leans his elbow on the stage. He purses his lips and sucks at her. She considers kicking his drink over, if not his face in, but decides if she got that close he'd probably drag her down by the ankle. She rips off her bottoms, all desire to entertain gone. She jigs grimly as far from him as she can get.

"Hey hey!" shouts Greasy, "look at that beautiful hunk of meat. Spread it for me, baby! Comeoncomeoncomeoncomeon! Over here, sweetheart, right in my face. Open up, baby. Come on, cunt! I'm not paying you to look at hair. You dirty cunt! You need someone to come up there and spread it for you? Open it, cunt."

"JOE!" yells Callie, "JOE!"

Joe trots out of the office, clapping.

"Just enjoying the show, man," says Greasy to Joe, throwing his hands back in the old "I'm clean" gesture.

"Yeah, well," mumbles Joe, "Fire regulations, clear stairs. You know these chicks. They're all a little . . . Go on, drink up, tell the girl the next one's on the house."

With a glare at Callie for dragging him out, he walks back to the office, clapping his hands.

Callie is sick. Literally sick. Clammy, nauseated. What can be wrong with me? Maybe I need some water. I didn't have time for a drink before I came up. I mean, so what? Just two more obnoxious drunks. Remember the Platonic honky-tonk, and how it's not their fault and—phooey! This is insane.

The two dudes are smiling at her. They've gotten to her, and they know it. It's a kind of rape.

She doesn't wait for her last song, she runs down and into the dressing room. She sits on a beer keg listening to the whoosh of the deodorant machine.

When she walks out the two dudes are gone, but so what? Nice or slimy, they all leave sooner or later, and others come, until it stops being people, just beers on stilts. Pleasant beers, depressing beers, and oh, such sad and lonely beers.

"Killed herself! Oh, I'm so sorry."

"Left you. I'm sorry to hear that."

"Only one leg. God, that's tough."

"Died. Oh, how that must have hurt."

Oh, I'm sorry about that, sorry, too bad, sorry—but the real sorry part is you stop being sorry. I mean make up your minds, guys, what do you want, pussy or sorry? This dude's handing you his guts on a tip tray, and the next one is trying to rent your ass for fifteen dollars, and they're both the same, inter-changeable, two phases of the same huge cosmic dirty joke.

"What's about six inches long with a head on it and drives women wild?"

"You say you just came back from Vietnam and your old lady ran off with the manager of a Kinny's shoe store?"

"Sex *la vive*, buddy."

"O.K., I'll fall for it. A penis?"

"No. A dollar. A dollar is about six inches long and has a head on it, and . . ."

"But not this kid, mister. Only quarters drive me wild."

No, aged spade, I do not want to live in your four-room mansion in San Jose. I want to wash these dirty ashtrays and get rid of my bank and get in my car and drive home, straddling the center strip because there're no other cars, so spaced on exhaustion it's like a rapture of the deeps, schools of semis swimming toward me with their red and green eyes.

When all the housewives and tellers and Brussels sprouts packers are fast alseep, Thunder zooms down the center of the highway, maneuvering like Sterling Moss, remembering those glorious days when she was the Old West's only dancing drag racer, humming the "William Tell Overture" as she goes, rump titty rump titty rump rump rump. Yes, the Lone Ranger, and it's hi-yo, Thunder!

Late one afternoon, a bunch of us—me, Button, Whitey, and Rudy, a regular who did carpentry —cruised next door to the Santa Clara County Animal Shelter. The bottoms of the windows were painted over, and there was so much dirt on them anyway the place had never seemed penetrable, just some blank structure attached to Obie's for ballast.

Whitey had the key, and we went inside. It looked as though it had been abandoned for years. But what kind of a business could you run next door to Obie's, with the boom-boom coming through the walls and hookers turning tricks outside your front door?

There was a counter running down one side, covered with little mouse turds, and another room straight back with rusty cages lying on the floor. A door in the back of the counter led through a storage area with a sink to a passage lined with cells for the animals. We went through a door at the end of the passage and found the outside runs attached to each cage. The little yard was concrete and ended in the back wall of a cleaning plant.

"What do you think?" Whitey asked me.

"Perfect."

Obie's Blue Palace "Swedish" Sinema was on its way.

Button ran around waving his hands. "We'll build a little loft here, see . . . the projection booth goes right here. . . . How about real dimmers for the lights just like in the movies? I can do that with no sweat . . . You know, Lise tells me she's done a little of this kind of work, just for the experience. . . ."

Rudy moved around silently with his tape measure.

Everyone figured the Sinema couldn't miss. Guys all primed by the live show could duck next door to beat off in peace in the dark. Guys who went to the Sinema first would be ready for a beer and something live to flesh out the movie.

Of course, it would probably make things rougher on the girls. Twice worked up, twice thwarted, their X-ray eyes now full of perversions, the movie-goers, rough with frustration, would be even harder to please. We'd probably have to resuscitate the Siren. But so it goes. Whitey figured three or four hundred a night gross, with only a doorman to pay, and that's enough to go through a lot of dancers.

Various people owned pieces of the enterprise, but Obie had put Whitey in complete charge, and he grew distant and nervous with responsibility. He was also getting started with Globe Presentations; one afternoon I stopped by the Shelter to check progress and found two nervous, naked chicks dancing to a transistor radio amid the plaster and paint cans. Pressed for time, Whitey was combining his activities: spackle and snatch.

The girls' minds were further blown by a parting warning not to breathe a word about the interview.

Whitey was afraid that if Prick-face and Fuck-face found out about this rival organization before it had enough clients, they would pull out all their girls, leaving Globe-A-Go-Go stranded. I envisioned worse things; going to the mattresses in the Animal Shelter; massacres against the whorehouse-orange walls; a territorial war like the Chicago gangs' over who got to supply the dancing girls to the west side of San Jose.

One night the movie supplier showed up at the bar, a soft, androgenous man with a voice like a mouthful of yoghurt. Every second word out of Peter's mouth was "quality"—you want quality; it depends on the quality; what quality show; it's all in the quality quality quality. He spent an hour in and out of the office and the Shelter, talking quality to Whitey in that clotted voice, paying absolutely no attention to the dancers, which seemed odd considering the behavior of our other suppliers. The two men who came to fix the floor behind the bar had spent most of their time on all fours tapping absently with hammers while they stared at the stage upside down through their legs; the man who came to fix the Coke dispenser stood transfixed in puddles of syrup; the carpet man lured all the girls over to feel the nap of his samples.

It didn't seem so odd after I'd seen what Peter was used to. He came back the next night with his equipment and set up the projector in the cold, paint-smelling concrete box. Whitey was there, and Button, Rudy, a couple of guys who were friends of Obie's, and Obie himself.

It took a long time to set up. Upside-down breasts flashed and disappeared. Music degenerated into lubulubulubulub. Obie sent me to get beer for

145

everybody. Rudy took out a screwdriver and finished bolting down some seats.

"You're gonna have to get some kind of heating in here," Obie said to Whitey. His voice echoed in the empty room.

When the movie finally got going the voices were out of sync. A man lolling on a blanket in the grass with his cock draped casually over his thigh said in a fluting voice, "Oh, don't! Mother will be here any minute."

The girl, in jeans, with her breasts draped casually over her arm, said in a bass, "Don't worry, Nancy. I can take care of your mother, heh heh."

Cut to a girl and a boy sitting on a car in the desert—cactus, sand. The girl is naked. The boy has a cowboy hat and levis.

The girl zips down his fly and extracts his root. I'd given up thinking I was smaller than everybody else several years ago, but this dude had me wondering again.

The strange thing about this scene is that the girl is looking off to the left of the screen, the boy to the right. Not once do they look at each other.

He reaches out, finds the nearest boob, and grabs.

The girl, staring resolutely westward, starts agitating her hand.

There's hoedown music playing in the background: "Turkey in the Straw."

The boy, free hand resting on his knee, honks the boob.

The girl has reached the stage where it looks like she's conducting "The Flight of the Bumblebee."

Cut back to the blanket. Mother, smartly turned out in jodhpurs and carrying a bullwhip, has just entered the corral and spotted her daughter, half naked, leaning over this low life, giggling.

"My *goo*ness, how come it's getting so big and *stee*-uf!"

"Howdy, ma'm," says the cowboy.

Mother goes for him with the whip. He grabs the end and pulls. She falls on top of them.

"Now I'll show you why my THING gets hard!" he says. "Help me hold your mother down."

"Don't you dare . . . oooooo . . . Nancy!"

"But Momma. You and Daddy always *tole* me . . ."

Deedle deedle dee deedle dum dum dee . . .

Nancy holds her mother's arms while the cowboy pulls off her jodhpurs. She twists and thrashes. Now she's trussed with her own bullwhip, her scarf tied around her face. The daughter is holding her legs apart. The cowboy bends over her. . . .

It's back to the car. The boy looks like sardines are repeating on him. If the girl had a violin bow in her hand instead of a cock she'd be doing a hot pizzicato. They both sit patiently on the hood, amidst the cacti, waiting for something to give.

Suddenly the girl looks straight at us, smiles, mouths words, and turns away scowling again. Probably something like "I hope to hell you remembered the film this time, Charlie."

Back at the corral, Big Daddy in a Stetson has just ridden up to find his gagged and bound wife being reamed with the handle of a bullwhip by his hired hand, who is reclining with one hand behind his head while the sixteen-year-old virgin daughter sucks him off.

This was a moment of heavy dramatic potential, but even Euripides would have had trouble with that hee-haw music jigging along in the background, and somehow the ensuing chase, with much whipping and leaps over the watering trough, didn't live up to it.

A true epiphany approached, however.

Back on the hood, we have switched to a close-up of the prick, bright purple and looking like an outraged planarian. The girl leans down, her hair blowing across her face.

Stop that goddam hoedown! They should be playing the Love-Death duet from *Tristan und Isolde*, and here's this dumb fucking goddam hoedown.

"Any idiot could do better than this," I panted to Whitey.

"You may get your chance," whispered the new Talent Coordinator of Globe Presentations.

The camera zoomed in. Suddenly I forgot the music. I thought about shots. The boy should get some shots right away, because it could be danger-ous being blown by a girl with rabies. Why else should she be foaming at the mouth. Unless they stopped the action and fed her a bottle of Jergen's Lotion. Surely that isn't—I mean oozing out of the sides of her mouth like that, dripping off her chin in long mozarella ropes, her Adam's apple working like the handle of a slot machine. The projector skips a few frames, and still it's coming, enough little people to populate China four times over.

Jesus! nobody creams that much, especially not some guy who hasn't moved a muscle in his face for the last half hour.

"Hey—is that for real?" croaked Button.

"Did I tell you quality or did I tell you quality!" Peter called out.

148

"Sure it's for real," said Obie. "You just don't notice when it's you getting the job."

I noticed. I noticed Mrs. Matteo, determined to fulfill her Older Woman Tutorial contract to the letter, almost choke to death and deposit on my belly a tiny pearly and translucent puddle. This stuff in the movie reminded me more of the day my brother, that righteous rebel, dramatized one morning in no uncertain terms that he was fed up with Cream of Wheat.

Or the taps at Obie's, sometimes, when you start a new keg, a stream of foam that stops, starts, stops, dribbles. . . .

Little Nancy was finally deflowered by a combination of her pissed-off mother, her father, who had fallen into confusion after a hit on the head, the hired hand, and Daddy's horse. It was all as nothing after that dazzling climax.

My only interest was how the separate parts of the plot would merge—Daddy, Mother, Nancy, Hand, Horse, Boy, and Girl—in some mad denouement.

At least the car could have driven past the corral.

But it ended unresolved, a shot of the blanket, a shot of the car, leaving my imagination with a hard-on. Maybe I should get into blue movies. For instance, if I'd been making the movie I would have had the radiator explode right at the crucial moment, blowing the hood up in the air with a terrific geyser of steam, everything foaming and gushing together, as the couple, still deadpan, flew off into the cactus.

At the very least I could play hoedown licks on my fiddle in the background.

We all blinked at each other in the light.

"That's quality, all right," said Whitey.

149

"What did I tell you?" said Obie. "Peter's a quality guy."

"Not only that—it's the *quality* of the quality . . . " said Button, petering off into reptilian reveries.

"Come and have a beer, Peter," said Obie. "This Peter, too. Lot's of Peters around here all of a sudden, ain't there."

Peters, Peters everywhere, and not a drop to . . .

Cut back to the bar, steamy, smoky, a dancer gyrating naked under the red light. Now on top of my X-ray eyes I have opthamoloscope vision. I look at the guys humping their beer mugs and see past the clothing, through the very flesh to the uretheter, winding like a snake up to sacs where ducts curled like refrigerator coils pump a white protein flood toward the foaming delta. . . .

"What's happening?" Callie asked me. Slate had been covering for me on the door.

"We were checking out the movie next door."

"Can you believe I'm thirty-four years old and I've never seen a dirty movie."

"I'm not sure you want to see one."

"I'm not, either."

But, of course, she finally did, one night before work, with Button happy for a chance to play with the equipment handling the projection, Callie and me alone down below.

It was a mistake. She didn't even last until the Big Cream.

"You and I don't know each other well enough to be watching something like this together," she said.

I felt embarrassed; a boy getting his hands slapped; then I was pissed off. Why did this cunt have to be so goddam serious about everything? She laid on all these heavyweight emotional trips like a young chick, uncompensated by a young body; she had the once-burned cautions of an older chick without the mellowness and lack of bullshit. She was neither fish nor fowl, an overworked, overweight, overgrown girl, tied down by a dead marriage, probably sexual as a flounder—what has she got anyhow?

Well, she's got possibilities.

And, let's face it, Stern: she's got you.

One night an old MG TC pulled into the parking lot. The driver strode up to the door and straight past me like he had some official business inside.

Callie was waiting by the door with a beer in her hand.

The dude stopped short like he'd hit a wall.

Callie started, upsetting beer down the front of his jacket. Then she turned and ran.

I took a good look at the dude. He wasn't any bigger than me, but heavyset. He gave the impression of being hidden—a full beard, hair low across his forehead. The contortion around his eyes wasn't out of place in a man with beer dripping down his fly, but I knew that wasn't it; and he was twisting at the beard right under his mouth, pushing it against his lip, balling the hair and flesh together in a compulsive rhythm.

"Grand . . . Central . . . Station!" I said to myself, thinking about the radio program when I was a kid: "Daily witness to a thousand unknown dramas," or something like that.

This guy stood for a while, kneading his mouth,

then he went and sat down at the bar. I didn't see Callie, but she'd have to surface when her turn came to dance.

I didn't like him showing up here, either. Up to now Mr. Calliope—who else?—was nobody to me. I didn't even know his name, and in my relentless efforts to be mothered by other people's wives I had determined that when the old man is always "my husband," never Jim or George, that's a good sign. A name is powerful; names conjure up their owners. I figured Callie didn't want him there with us, didn't want him to exist for me.

But there he was in front of me, real, even suffering, and also outweighing me by thirty or forty pounds.

The music had stopped.

"NEXT!" yelled the manager, clapping his hands. "Come on—who's up?"

He finally tried the dressing room. In a minute he came out with Callie. He gave her a pat on the rump toward the jukebox. After a while he came over to the door.

"These cunts," he said. "One's dingier than the next. This one's in the dressing room putting her clothes on. Says she's got a stomach-ache. I told her, 'Listen, honey, you run out on me in the middle of a shift, you don't have to bother coming back.' I tell you, there are nights when my ulcer's so bad I belong in bed. You don't see me hiding in no corner crying about it."

Calliope was up on stage, as uncoordinated as her very first time. She kept squinting into the audience but her eyes were too bad to spot where he was, and after the second dance she just looked straight in front of her and said, "Please go away. Please just get out of here. I'm asking you, please. Go home."

"NOT UNTIL YOU DROP YOUR PANTIES, SWEETHEART!" yelled somebody in a drunken voice, getting a few laughs.

Now was the time for the guy to push through the crowd to the stage, yelling:

"I WILL NOT ALLOW THE MOTHER OF MY CHILDREN TO SHAKE HER BACKSIDE IN FRONT OF A BUNCH OF DRUNKEN BAR-FLIES!" The manager had been having it entirely too easy this evening.

Instead, after he watched her do one number with her pants off, he split. I probably imagined the once-over he gave me on the way out.

Callie finished her set, got down off the stage, and started running around looking for him. She ended up at the door, peering into the parking lot. I told her the guy she was uptight about had left. I put my arm around her. She grabbed my shoulders and leaned against me.

I knew it didn't mean all that much. There are times when you simply need to touch something warm and sentient, it helps remind you you're still there. She and Libby used to do it for each other. Libby wasn't around any more; I'd fill the bill.

Still, I almost asked her if she'd stay tonight—"You don't have to go home if you don't want to" kind of thing, at least as much reassurance as proposition. I held back, though.

This wasn't any one-night stand. She wouldn't, like Annie, just conveniently disappear. It might really tear things with the old man if she left him hurting this particular night; I could end up with her and two kids, in my single at Toomy's Transient Hotel, one of which would wake up and want to play each of the hundred times a night my ancient neighbor flushed the ancient and equally noisy communal toilet.

Or more likely she says Thank you just the same, Peter, and I've shot my bolt on a false decision —tonight it's not a question of desire but of loyalty, she owes it to the guy out of common compassion, which is evidently one of her long suits anyhow, to go home and have it out about what she's doing here.

Come to think of it, maybe what she's doing here, maybe this whole bottomless gig was only a way to make him react in the first place; Sandy Matteo told me a few incredible things she'd done along those lines, on summer days in Central Park. Right now Callie probably didn't know she was doing it—next time, like Mrs. Matteo, she would.

Anyhow, remembering the time I lived with Lady Linda, I was willing to bet after they'd screamed at each other for a while Callie didn't end up sleeping on the couch.

I wasn't so much jealous of him fucking her as I was of the emotional bond. Even hurting each other is something between two people. And if I had the thing psyched out right, more than that. She must really love the guy to go through all this for him. "Together in our hearts . . ." Man, she *told* you. She's not pulling any games with you.

Callie is all right. Not sure what she wants, scared and confused, but a straight shooter. The kind some other dude has *always* got. Fuck it.

I started thinking about the doors I could knock on after work and stand a chance of getting in. But after the night was over and I was walking back to the hotel I forgot it all. It's so fine walking, all alone, down three-a.m. streets, even in San Jose.

For a week the Sinema was packed with Obie's partners and cronies getting private showings. There was a second movie now, too, a more clinical sixty-nine-positions-illustrated deal, and they'd sit in there all night drinking beer and hooting and running the two half-hour flics over and over.

The night the Sinema officially opened there were three customers the whole night. The next night there were five, two the next, four, seven, three. That's how it went. No sweat. Everyone agreed it would take a while for word to spread, and maybe five dollars for forty-five minutes' worth of movies was a little too much, but lowering the price right away was as good as announcing they weren't worth the money, or, to put it another way, when you're dealing with quality it's a quality move to charge quality prices. All Obie did after a disastrous two weeks was to tell Whitey to replace Slate as ticket-taker with a pretty girl.

The pretty girl, after lots of lobbying from Gerry and pleading phone calls from Berkeley, turned out to be Libby. She must have left home again, or was lying through her teeth, because she started coming six times a week and half the time she stayed over.

They gave her a roll of tickets like mine and put her behind the little counter with shelves in front that were empty now, but Whitey planned to fill with the same kind of skin rags and sex-novelty items they sold in machines in the men's room.

I hadn't realized what an attractive girl Libby was. Her hair gleamed, her forehead was high and pure as a madonna, and she always looked so clean she seemed to neutralize the rancid vibes surrounding her. Her speaking voice was low and mellow, and her rich, rueful little laugh, about ten years older than the rest of her, was a promising crack in that jujyfruit California blond façade.

She and Gerry hung out over the counter for a few nights, then suddenly the big romance seemed to be off. Gerry's GTO resumed its old slot at the motel office and Libby went into a heavy spade thing. Three or four black exquisites were always doing the Funky Penguin in front of the counter. She started saying "Shee-ut, man" and slurring her g's. It even looked as if her ass was developing more soul.

One night she came over to the door and told me, "Man, you should have seen mah mamma when Ah come home one weekend with Benny? You know Benny, cat with the white El Dorado? and I go, 'Momma, this here is mah new boy friend, Benny,' and Benny, you know his sense of humor, he goes . . ."

Yes, I knew Benny's sense of humor, which ran to scooping the foam off his beer onto the front of his pants, grabbing the nearest girl and yelling, "Momma, you see what you make me do to myself? Shee-ut, girl, who gonna pay for my cleaning bill! . . ."

I pictured a home in the Berkeley Hills, eucalyptus and pine and glass views of the whole Bay, two foreign cars in the carport and Libby's old DeSoto parked in the drive just sort of emphasizing the whole trip by contrast. Standing at the door in rich grainy threads is Mrs. Fenton, who has been bludgeoned into promising she'll stop interfering—"Otherwise you'll never see me again, Mother, I mean it"—seeing, and perhaps it's better not to see after all, the snotty but much loved princess of this castle, eighteen years old, arrive with Benny, big black Benny, in his white Cadillac and wool beret with the outsize pompon, old foam-bulge bopping and jiving down the driveway . . .

"But Gerry's still my true love," Libby confided. "He just doesn't know his own mind"—which I translated to mean that Libby wanted to do a heavy number and Gerry wanted to be free to sleep where he wanted.

I think the spades were supposed to help Gerry learn his mind by filling it with jealous Southern rages, but when that didn't happen she upped the stakes. Barflies of any complexion couldn't cut it against the main competition, which, despite Gerry's forays into the ranks of the dancers, was still Paula. You couldn't beat the general manager's mother with anything less than Obie himself, or Whitey, or Button, somebody heavy-duty. The logic of her situation made it inevitable.

Slate.

Slate exposed the most outside and the least inside of anyone at Obie's. The sheer size of him made this reserve seem natural, as if the normal human effects didn't concern him. He was more like a very intelligent animal, a lion, charming in his lion way, a moral and emotional blank.

The only personal thing he ever said to me was, "I come from the raisin country." That, I figured, must be some place like the Napa Valley, but I never took it geographically. Raisin Country struck me as a special land, like something out of the Wizard of Oz, a land of raisin-colored giants.

The feeling I got from Slate reminded me of a bully I courted when I was in public school. The kid accepted my skinny attentions, but I'd seen him turn on other of his friends, and my dread gave a strange quality to my laughter. I found myself laughing like that around Slate.

Yet he was a perfectly good-natured dude. He loved to tell jokes and fool with his cars. With men waving pool sticks and throwing tantrums all over the place, I never even heard him raise his voice. But he scared the shit out of me. It wasn't just his size. It was that he recognized no authority. The manager ordered everyone else around. Slate he cajoled. Even Obie deferred to him. Being so big probably helps develop this kind of attitude, but I've run into a few normal-size cats that had it, too. They're dangerous people.

One night I went over to the Sinema to stretch my legs, and found Libby with a bruise the color of the wall on her white, white forehead. It seemed Slate wanted to ball and she didn't and he threw her down and she hit her head and he put his hand over her face until she couldn't breathe enough to struggle any more, and then he raped her.

"Sweet mother of God, where was this? In Berkeley?"

"At the motel. His room."

"What the hell were you doing in his room if you didn't want to ball him?"

"Shee-ut, Peter, it's all just jive. I been to Stick's apartment, I been with Benny five, six times, I even slept one night on the couch at his old lady's house. I mean you tell a person you just want to jive around and have fun, that should be the end of it. I mean he raped me, Pete—he fucking *raped* me!"

I suppose it served her right. She was gaming on him and he called her on it. But still . . .

"Why don't you go home, Libby. Why the hell do you hang around this dump anyhow?"

"Believe me, my home is no better. My older sister split when she was sixteen, things were so crummy. My parents fight all the time, my mother has a psychiatrist on twenty-four hour emergency call, the usual middle-class melodrama. I've got to get out of there before I go crazy, and I'd rather do this than be a file clerk somewhere for a lousy buck sixty-five an hour."

But then we had a visit from the Fire Marshal. When he left there was a notice on the door of the Sinema that said premises were unsafe for occupancy until further notice, by order of the San Jose Fire Department, and Libby was out of a job.

It was no big loss to anyone but Libby. The place hadn't made more than fifty dollars in the three weeks it was open. Obie and his partners preferred, for right now, a good tax write-off to laying out for new sprinklers.

Libby still hung around San Jose. We had a new manager, she had a fake I.D., and everyone else looked the other way. She sat in the corner of the bar, smoking cigarettes, surrounded by half a dozen flat beers that hopeful customers had the bar girls bring her. Once or twice when a girl didn't show, the manager let her dance, that same sweet-ass thump thump jiggle, except no more joking around and hot pants, sssssss. The dudes got off on her anyhow, yelled "LET'S SEE WHAT YOU GOT!" and "SPREAD IT, BABY!" only nobody in the know at Obie's so much as raised an eyebrow in her direction. She belonged to Slate, want to or not.

Slate continued to paw all the girls, not more than once or twice a night, not enough to get them really frantic, but enough to keep his rights established. He did the same thing to Libby, but simply more often, systematically, matter-of-factly, they way you handle a new baseball glove to break it in.

I don't know where she slept the nights he didn't want her—maybe on Benny's old lady's couch. A few nights she curled up and went to sleep in the projection booth of the condemned Sinema. Otherwise I watched her go off with Slate, a child next to his huge bulk, back to the motel where she could see her true love across the court going into Paula's or ushering laughing dancers into his room.

And where he could see her stepping out of the Coupe De Ville.

Damn, you have to give it to these chicks. Libby had a lot of her mother's balls. She'd gone ahead with the Slate trip, rape and all, and it finally worked. She and Gerry started huddling in corners again. Just before it became inevitable that Gerry would presently have his balls handed to him on a tip tray, they made the announcement. Libby and Gerry had rediscovered true love, and they were getting married.

Nothing else short of shooting him would have

Callie mentioned to one of our regulars who worked at the station across the street that she was looking for a used car. A few weeks later he told her he had something lined up, a '67 VW in good condition. Callie didn't know anything about conditions in VW's, and she wondered if I would do her the big favor of popping across the street to look at it.

We made a date to pop the next morning. I got up at ten, the first time I'd been up before noon in another long time. It was a windy day. Clouds covered and uncovered the sun. The pennants on the car lots made whipping sounds all down the street. Even San Jose looked clean and brisk.

I had breakfast at Sambo's, feeling strange eating ham and eggs at the exotic hour of ten in the morning. I walked to the gas station, swinging my arms, aware that the only exercise I got these days was strolling around in the dead of night.

Across the street from the station was Obie's, shut up tight. At this distance all that stood out was the white square of the condemnation on the door of the Sinema.

It looked small, insignificant, a gray concrete box with a dead neon sign hard to read in the sun.

I looked the car over, an old blue warrior with one green fender and a funky homemade wooden bumper, but it started right up and sounded good.

Callie came around eleven, out of breath: "I hitched! It was terrible! Hello! I'm sorry!"

I'd never seen her in a dress before. In fact this was the first time I had seen her in broad daylight. Her hair looked lighter in the sun, like cotton candy.

She squinted up at me, the smile washing her mouth like clouds. I felt a little uncertain myself. At night the roles were defined. Out in the morning we were rather ambiguous strangers.

We pulled through it by concentrating on tires and transmissions, and as soon as we got in the car and it turned out Callie had never driven a floor shift before, I was safely ensconced in the neutral position of driving instructor.

I took her across the street, and she drove around Obie's parking lot. After an hour she was still stalling all over the place. "I know I don't have much natural ability," she said, "but I think I might be better if we weren't going around in circles at Obie's. The symbolism is distracting."

So I checked with the guy at the station, and I checked with Callie, and I checked with the sunshine and headed south onto the freeway to set Callie loose on the up-shift down-shift hills of Santa Cruz.

We opened the sun roof and the wind fluttered through at aeronautic frequencies. It felt just like a small plane, skimming over the tops of fir trees. Callie lugged and overrevved enthusiastically, stoked on the bug after the big heavy Jaguar. It didn't seem the day could grow any brighter until we reached the end of town and found the ocean, silver and crennelated like the skin of a fish.

We got out of the car and stood on a cliff looking down at the water. The wind was fierce. Every once in a while it dropped for a moment, leaving us stunned in pockets of warmth like currents in a cold lake.

I turned and kissed Callie on the lips, lightly. A taste of warmth as sudden as no wind, but mostly my own hair blowing across our faces.

She reached up and brushed my hair back. I touched her head and it felt just like petting the Airdale we had when I was a kid. I laughed and hugged her.

"Goodness, but you're a kind person, Peter," she said.

"Let's climb down to the beach," I said, not feeling at all kind.

"I'll never make it. In addition to fainting, I also get vertigo."

"It's not as steep as it looks. I'll go first."

Without waiting I started down. There was a skinny dirt path through the ice plant, but it was so steep it dropped out of sight below me. I wiggled down, holding on to the ice plant, till I came to a ledge. Without twisting around, all I could see was ice plant above me and ocean below; the overhang hid the beach. The ocean seemed to be lapping right up against the cliffs, nothing but ocean straight up to the sky.

A familiar feeling, voluptuous and sad, came over me. My own skin was the walls of an isolation chamber. I hung over the ocean, rocking the lonely and familiar emotion.

"Peter! Where are you!"

I stood up. Callie was still at the top, hugging herself against the wind.

"Peter, I can't. I'm afraid."

"Just down to me. The view is terrific."

She started down. Pebbles and dirt slid under her feet and bounced around me. She moved like a person who doesn't know where the center is, overbalancing, shifting her weight the way she did the car, too soon, too late. She stopped and looked back up a lot, but she kept on coming. A few feet away she saw the ledge sticking out into nothing and froze, grabbing at the ice plant.

"Peter, I can't. Help me!"

"Take it easy. Wiggle your butt into the plants. I'll cover you on this side."

She shifted around, bracing her feet on the rocks. She rested on her back in a hollow of ice plant. I came up beside her on the downhill side.

From this angle there was no ocean at all, just froth running in and out of little arches in the cliff wall, wetting the beach and disappearing again. It felt snug after the ledge, a nest of flowers and spikes that crunched, no wind, and the hot, spicy smell of succulent.

"Are you still scared?" I put my hand over her heart. She was. Still, one hand released its death grip on the ice plant and moved over to cover mine.

I felt her relax, little by little, through the palm of my hand. I was perfectly content. In a few minutes I could roll over and press her deep into the spikes; I could also just lie here, fingering the lambswool through to the scalp, learning her ear and the side of her face. We were released, free of gravity, riding a space capsule of purple flowers wheeling through a blue sky. There was nothing wrong we could say or do. I'd never had this sensation before, but I recognized it.

"How I'd love to live some place like this. That's my dream. A little house by the ocean."

I agreed from twenty years experience that living by the ocean was a fine thing. Then we just lay there, so still and peaceful that a tiny wild cottontail browsed its way past us through the succulents a few feet below.

"I don't know what's going to happen," she said peacefully after a while.

"I do. Sooner or later."

"My goodness. No place like this, at least, I hope."

"Why not? With a climactic nine-hundred foot fall onto the sand."

"I wouldn't mind that—the fall, I mean. The sand looks so soft. I bet it feels so good on your feet. If I wasn't such a chicken I'd finish climbing down and take all my clothes off. I'd like to dance around and let the wind clean all that smoke and dirt out of my pores."

"Listen! Those are seals."

"I feel so good. This is so silly."

Her bare legs were covered with goose bumps, and I covered them with mine to keep them warm. But pretty soon we were both shivering, and we made our way back up the path, Callie hanging on to the back of my jacket.

She almost drove over the cliff trying to find reverse, but she didn't make a single wrong move on the way back to town; the magic was still with us.

Putting off San Jose, we stopped for something at a big lunch counter with lots of hippies around the door. As soon as we got inside the mood vanished.

back, and we were hit unexpectedly by that familiar yeasty smell. It was an honest-to-god bar, the kind I'd almost forgotten about; a guy handed me a beer over the bar and I gave him a quarter for it, a straight manly transaction, no bullshit. The beer was ice cold, and you could obviously sit all day over one glass if you felt like it. The music was just loud enough to keep the conversation company. People floated in and out, all sunshine heads, clean, embroidered, elaborately gentle. Still, it was a bar, and outside a big garden room was covered with mirrors from floor to ceiling. Maybe it was the mirrors. Maybe because it was close to three.

"Let's not talk about Obie's," we said in unison, and laughed, but it was uptight laughter. My mind started chasing in circles again. "Kind," was I? Sure, very kind to listen to you sound off about the work because you need to unload all that shit so you can keep on swallowing it, all for some other guy. Today was a little payment on account. You know what you have to do to keep me listening. We'll make a deal. Your cunt, my attention.

As we walked out to drive back to San Jose, I saw us in the mirrors: a big woman in a green dress, a tall skinny dude with wind in his hair.

Libby broke up with Gerry again. This time the reason was Lise.

Button was still pushing his courtship, but his Maturely-Dashing-Blade-Trifling-at-the-Stage-Door number was wearing thin. In addition to handling all the girls' cases, he'd rewired the taps, installed a black light on stage, fixed the amplifiers, and overhauled the jukebox. He had no excuse to hang around, he just hung, paying for his beers like anybody else, reduced to the status of regular.

When Lise's car threw a rear wheel bearing he got down on his pearl-gray knees in the puddles of Ripple and grease to check it out. While the car was being fixed, he taxied Lise back and forth to the vet with the snakes, who were having a hard winter.

"I go back down south very soon," Lise pronounced with as much emphasis as a weather report.

"I love that Hungarian sense of humor," chuckled Button desperately. "You know you're not going anywhere, my little goulash. You're staying right here at Obie's, to make us all happy."

"Very soon," Lise smiled, and while Button hung

around the door with Slate and me, beer glass in hand, leading every topic around to her with elaborate casualness, Lise turned her steamy eyes on Libby.

I saw them sitting together at the end of the bar, Lise describing something with her hands, Libby laughing with her head back.

Sitting at the other end with the pool players, Gerry watched them.

As Gerry often said, "Ah want to taste it *owl*, Ah want to try *every*thang life has to give," which is why, I imagine, as Libby told me the next morning, she and Gerry ended up in Lise's room that night after work, passing a bottle of bourbon around until Libby just passed out. They were all laughing about having to put Libby to bed like a baby, and it really was funny how her arms and legs just flopped around when they tried to take her clothes off, but then she was naked, on top of the bed, and it was just Lise, *fondling* her.

"Gerry, for God's sake do something," Libby cried, suddenly sobering up.

Gerry was sprawled in the chair, his shirt open, his mouth loose, drunk as a skunk.

"Just take it easy, dahlin', just relax," he said absently, looking, looking.

Libby struggled, which didn't get her anywhere. Eventually she was penetrated, how or by whom she didn't know. Later it was dark, and she was crawling over miles of knees to reach the side of the bed. After she was sick she fell asleep again, and when she woke up she was alone.

In their big glass tank on the dresser, the snakes were waiting for breakfast in great, silent agitations.

Libby got me out of bed at the hotel that morning,

looking about twelve years old and very sick. I told her to get into bed. "Do we have to do anything?" she said, not protesting the idea, just wondering. I could have climbed in next to her and fucked her any way I wanted. She was perfectly demoralized.

I heated water on my gas ring and made instant coffee. Libby cooled hers by crying into it. I agreed that Gerry was the lowest skunk in creation to just sit around watching Lise take advantage of her like that. I didn't tell her what I thought; that the whole thing was planned, that Gerry handed Libby over to Lise for a return favor: to be able to claim to be the only dude at Obie's who ever got a piece of that sapphic Hungarian pussy.

If I ever need to get back at Gerry, I'll tell him what he got.

After a while, between sobs, Libby found her giggle again. "I'm just dumb, I guess. I just let these things happen. Shee-ut, that place must have turned me into a nymphomaniac or something."

Libby looked far out, her big brown eyes all teary and her skin hot with crying. I liked Libby. I reminded myself that eighteen was more my turf than thirty-four.

"Get your ass into the bathroom and clean yourself up before I make you prove that last statement," I said. After a shower and another cup of coffee she split, hung around somewhere, I guess, until twelve, and went back to the bar. Where else did she have?

But the bar taketh away and the bar giveth. That night she had a new drinking companion: Obie's resident reformer, Father Killam.

I remember what a jolt it was seeing this dude for the first time, with the turned-around collar and the black suit and the red light haloing his snowy white hair, sitting right in the middle of the front row.

A priest! What next?

The snowy hair had nothing to do with the surprise. I was used to that. We had our nightly quota of gummers and tremblers pissing in their pants while the young dudes came in theirs. The girls were good to them, because they usually tipped and didn't grab, except once in a while for old time's sake. They all tended to come on the same days, and I finally figured it must have been something to do with when the Social Security checks came in.

They showed up on crutches, wheel chairs, canes, taking one step per minute hand over hand along the backs of chairs, the bar, convenient shoulders, anything. I wasn't sure if I was encouraged or put off by all this obscenile activity.

Once a guy slipped me a couple of bucks to make sure everybody was good to his old dad, out on his eighty-second-birthday spree. Pops, in a suit and bedroom slippers, sat in front for two hours, nodding off now and then, and every time the girls changed stages we just picked him up in his chair and plunked him down across the room.

Another time it was the kid's birthday, and his seventy-five-year-old father was throwing the party. Dad, a good deal fitter than his two middle-aged sons, got good and drunk and leaned over to snatch at the dancers' ankles.

"It's my baby's birthday," he kept yelling. "He's thirty-four years old. This is my baby."

The baby, a tired-looking man with gray in his hair, kept chanting back, "Seventy-five years old! Can you believe it? Seventy-five years old, and none of us can keep up with him!"

"My wife's name is Lillian," the old man announced. "I have seven grandchildren and two great-grandchildren. This is my baby. He's thirty-four years old today."

"Seventy-five years old! Can you believe it?"

"This is my baby . . ."

Father Killam showed up a few times a month, always bought one beer, and watched one complete show, clapping politely. Then he'd spend the rest of the time trying to persuade whichever girl looked ripest for it to abandon this bottomless Sodom and come to God.

I was never sure about Killam. At first I thought he was a plainclothesman with a devious mind. Then I found out he was a real priest at a church called Saint Stephen's. This didn't guarantee his motives; old priests get as weird as the rest of us, no doubt. Finally I went back to my first idea. Killam was a kind of Vice, only on the God Squad.

I'm glad it was Killam and not one of the pimps. Libby was wiped out and ready for anything. I imagine it happens just like that with a lot of girls. By the time the chick's off her bummer she's broken in and what the hell. For a dancer it's easy. She's used to being paid for taking her clothes off.

Libby went the other way.

"Peter, it's just wonderful!" she said. "Since I got Jesus I stopped fornicating and cussing and smoking—I didn't even try, they just all fell away from me."

"How the hell can you get Jesus at Obie's?"

"Jesus," she said with great dignity, "can see beyond appearances. Anyhow, I won't be around here much longer. Father Killam is arranging for me to live with some friends of his in Santa Clara. It's a good Christian family, and they'll look after me like a

173

daughter. Father Killam says I should start thinking about going to college."

She sounded a little like a prerecorded announcement, but no denying the change was for the better. And so wise, little girl, so true. Why shouldn't Jesus come to Obie's?

Obie's before all else, in fact, this spiritual disaster area, this rehearsal for worse things to come complete with lurid lighting effects, flames, cannisters of brimstone, the groans and maniac howls of the suffering and, most of all, the eternal and everlasting frustration, which Dante, my expert, says is the real torment of hell—everything else being just the Devil's sense of show biz.

Dante also found out you have to dive right down there to be born again, and maybe that's why we're all here. Sex really isn't the point at all. The sex is a come-on and a cover-up, something to make it socially acceptable. We're really all here sinking down down down down down, like the song says, and we have our Beatrices too, tired sweaty ladies shambling around on a stage, going down down down down so we can all start up again. . . .

HMMMMMMMMMMM! I hear this heavenly Charlton Heston inspiration music interspersing the boom boom: "Lak a sex-a machine" —HMMMMMMMMMM! "I say HOT pants"— HMMMMMMMMMMMMM! Just like the sign says, COMING, "LIVE" FROM L.A., City of Angels. He's in plain clothes, of course, a carpet salesman in an iridescent suit or, shee-ut, maybe a brother in a white suede jumper over an orange silk blouse. Suddenly, the jukebox is a choir of angels, singing out the truth, the same old songs turned anagogical: I am drowning, drowning in a sea of love. . . . You

174

got to go down down down down down. . . . I was slipping into darkness. . . . I got what you need. . . . Turn to me. . . .

"WHERE IS MY GOOD SERVANT OBADIAH?" comes a voice. "AND WHERE IS MY DOORMAN PETER?"

Around the time she got her car, Callie, and Obie's, entered a Golden Era. For a brief time the glitter outshone the tarnish. Globe Presentations, the Sinema, Snowy Ayala, the specialities, Obie's Bottomless Marching Band, all climaxed by the go-go event of the decade: the Bottomless Wedding.

It was all coming together for Callie, too. She'd dropped about thirty pounds. After the first fifteen came off by themselves, she went at it with a vengeance. Her coital humps lofted, the dudes drooled, and only I, with my head against the lattice, could hear her counting out the pushups:

One-two-three-four, *One*-two-three-four.

She lay on her back and lowered her legs langorously. Her back was to the audience, and only I could see her eyes popping out of her head, her fists clenching nine *ten!* and with a sigh she let her feet touch the floor.

She touched her toes with her back to the audience; she camouflaged the knee bends with temple-goddess hand movements. She could have showed up in track shoes and done laps up there; nobody would have noticed so long as she gave a wiggle every mile or so.

She got tired of all the songs on the jukebox, and like a true seven-year veteran of the footnote did research in the record section of the library.

"Have you ever heard of someone called Otis Redding?" she asked me on her way in one night. "Is he ever good!"

Callie "discovered" B.B. King, Little Milton, King Curtis, Otis Sphann, Chuck Berry. Then—I could see her browsing on to the next section of the library—Bob Wills, Hank Williams, Flatt and Scruggs.

She came in one night with a stack of old forty-fives from the Goodwill and persuaded the manager to put them in. He cracked open the neon box, squatting against the wall with its ancient photo of Elvis Presley.

I'd never seen the jukebox opened before. I almost expected the demons to fly out, like Pandora's box, but, *mirabile dictu,* a pure, unearthly light flooded forth, bright as an arc lamp. The customers next to it threw up their hands and scuttled out of reach like morlocks, while Callie stood there, outlined in white light.

Then we were treated to music the likes of which Obie's had never heard: quivery Texas ballads, Oakie wails, hot licks, rock 'n' roll.

Callie really had her shit together up on stage. She was a terrific mime, with her big mobile features, and she acted out the songs. Sometimes she made fun of the whole trip, exaggerating bumps and grinds, stopping and staring right back at the cunt zombies, wiggling her fingers in her ears at them upside down when they yelled, "TURN AROUND AND DO THAT, BABY!"

"What do you think about while you're doing that?" someone yelled at her as Callie wiggled athletically on an imaginary penis (two-three-four-one . . .)

She answered immediately, "Recipes."

"Hah?"

"I'm thinking about making lasagne."

"How do you do that, sweetheart?"

"Well," she yelled, not missing a stroke of her Canadian Air Force Training Abdomen Flattener, "first I take some olive oil and I cut up some garlic . . ."

She flopped down and did a few seconds breathing technique, hahahahahahahahah, ". . . then I chop! hahahahahahahaha, the parsley . . ."

When girls get weary, and young girls do get weary . . .

"Two-three-four-orégano!"

"TAKE IT OFF!"

BASIL!

SPREAD!

SIMMER!

Along about the ricotto cheese, she turned on her back and lowered her panties to the count of ten.

"Wait till I do the chicken soup!" she yelled through the lattice. "I'll drive them wild!"

Callie was turning out more exotic than anything L.A. ever sent us: a bottomless dancer with a sense of humor.

She also toughened up a little. She stopped apologizing every time her ass got in the way of somebody's hand, and one time when some dude was giving her a hard time over his change I saw her take the quarter off the tip tray and flip it casually into his beer.

She started getting her own regulars, guys who came in mainly to see her: a gawk who drove a new Porsche and kept asking her to go on champagne cruisers up the Sacramento; a good-looking spade dude who came in every night at midnight when he got off work and told her what fun they could have together in Trinidad; a hippy type who tipped her a dollar a time and came in one night with a shirt he'd hand-lettered for her on the back in ornate script *KALI*. In the box was a card on which he'd written:

DIVINE MOTHER KALI

She is my mother
She is my father
She is my brother
She is my lover
She is my sun

She is my moon
She is my child
She is the grass
She is the dew

Look at how much she can teach
Her tongue dripping blood
A circle of skulls around her neck
A dagger in one hand
Giving birth in the other
The whole process of nature
How exquisitely subtle

"Peter, I didn't have the heart to tell him he put me in the wrong myth. It's interesting, though. Hardly anyone ever gets my name right, but this is the first time anyone's ever thought I was named after a Hindu goddess of destruction."

Oddest of all, though, was the courtship of Slate.

Callie wasn't at all his type—Slate liked his women petite and catatonic—but he started hanging around outside every night just to grab her as she stepped out of the VW.

"When you going to stop all this fooling and come with me? Why you want to go driving around in a little piece of grasshopper shit like that when you know what you got waiting for you?"

He indicated his latest Coupe De Ville, the Coupe Della Coupe of Coupe De Villes, a twenty-two-feet-from-front-fender-to-fin-fifty-nine Filmore cruiser.

"When I love someone, I buy them the *world.*"

Callie was as tactful as she could be about it, admiring the electric radio antenna and automatic dimmer, and even suggesting some enthusiasm for the proposition except, of course, sex *la vive.* She was married.

"Well, so what, powder puff? So am I."

"You socking it to that girl?" he asked me ominously one night. It was the one time I was glad I wasn't.

Sooner or later. It seemed to me she'd agreed. I wasn't pushing things. I didn't want her to think I was just another slob after a look up her cunt; not because I wasn't, but because I figured haste would be counterproductive to the final goal. But it was time for the move. The competition was building up. Even Gerry, who once told me he thought Callie was one of the *ugliest* things he ever saw, asked her back to the motel. He was stunned when she refused.

Then an opportunity arose that was tailor-made for my special advantages.

Isaac Stern was coming to San Francisco.

"You ever been married?" Gerry asked me one night.

"No."

"Neither have Ah. They say it's the shits. Well, what the hell, Ah've done just about everything else."

Thus did I learn of the reconciliation that would result in the biggest excitement at Obie's since the fire in the bathroom: Gerry and Libby Lou's bottomless wedding.

The wedding itself wasn't bottomless. Respectably covered by a white mini-dress and long white plastic boots, Elizabeth Louise Fenton was married to Mr. Gerald Wayne Ducoty at ten o'clock in the morning on the nineteenth of May at Saint Stephen's Episcopal Church. Then the real rites got under way at Obie's.

I hadn't seen much of Libby after she left my room that day. Her conversion seemed serious enough; at least I know she moved in with the good Christian family. But I guess Saint Stephen's as a hangout left something to be desired after Obie's, and the good

Christian family expected her to do a lot of house-work. So, Mrs. Gerald Wayne Ducoty told me afterward with her rich chuckle, she drove back to San Jose one day, collared Gerry at the motel, and said, "I'm sick of all this fucking around. You know we share true love. Let's get married."

Gerry had just been wiped out by a foxy dancer named Patti whom he'd been after for two weeks. I imagine the novelty of Libby's proposal appealed to him, too. Getting married at a bottomless bar to a ticket-taker at a porny movie house had to be even more far out than fucking a Lesbian Hungarian snake charmer.

Obie's was galvanized by the news. The girls, connubial disasters though they were—almost all of them were supporting no-good old men while they reared kids whose fathers had long since skipped on down the tracks—still went into a collective romantic transport. One of Obie's partners, who owned a piece of a liquor store, offered champagne at cost. Obie was paying for all the booze and food. This benevolence wasn't entirely out of character; at least two news-papers were sending people, and the publicity was cheap at the price. He'd probably also demand the *droit de seigneur,* or at the very least have holes drilled through the walls of Gerry's room while the party was going on, so he and his friends could watch later.

Whitey's contribution was entertainment, in the form of Obie's Bottomless Marching Band.

Whitey wasn't taking any chances of a showdown with the agency until he'd signed up every third female in San Jose. In the meantime, he decided to concentrate on a few specialties, like, say, an all girls' bottomless basketball team, the San Jose Globe

Twaters, or an Obie's baseball team, the Santa Clara County Master Batters. The Bottomless Band was to be the first, marching far and wide—Gilroy, Los Gatos, Salinas—under the banner of Globe Presentations, Clinton ("Whitey") Pringle, Talent Coordinator, and Peter ("Pete") Stern, Musical Director.

We had a week to rehearse and two musicians: Pat, who played the accordion, and Callie, the granddaughter of the lady with the crush on Galamian. I had my reservations. A cello in a marching band? How do you march with a cello? And what good is a cello in a bottomless band anyhow? All you'd see is cello with two knees and two arms sticking out around it. But none of the other girls played anything. So how could you have a marching band without a cello?

At our one get-together, *sans* instruments, all we accomplished was deciding whether it was necessary to rehearse bottomless. Whitey insisted it was, to get accustomed. Pat said she'd quit: "Ain't nobody I don't want to sees my cunt on my own time. You want to pay me my four an hour for the rehearsals, O.K. Otherwise, get fucked."

It was finally decided the girls could keep their clothes on except for dress rehearsals.

Libby bought Gerry a huge topaz in a platinum setting, and Gerry retaliated with a gold band set with nineteen diamond chips. "You all can count them," he told everybody, amazed at his own magnificence.

The rings were exchanged at the ceremony. I wasn't there, only Whitey for Gerry and Kathy for Libby, and one relative, Libby's sister Anita. Gerry's parents were in Alabama, where they could rot as far as he was concerned, and Libby's parents were evidently too busy engaging in the battle engendered by her father giving his permission over her mother's dead body. Gerry at least was white, he may have figured.

While Gerry and Libby were exchanging their "Ah dews," Paula and the girls were decorating the bar. They spread white cloths over the bar and the little counters around the stages. They covered the pool table and put the presents on it. Paula taped white crepe-paper streamers around the ceiling and stood on a barstool tying up balloons.

The liquor truck came, and I helped carry the champagne inside. Leroy and his two waitresses arrived and started setting up the wedding breakfast. The helpers decided they deserved an early start on the champagne. A cork flew across the bar and bounced off the ceiling.

The guests started arriving. Snowy with two beautiful chicks; Benny and Stick with their old ladies; several Joes emeritus; the gas-station gang; Fuck-face and Prick-face; Pornography Pete, Slate, with two large; sullen offspring, Ralph down from Burlingame; Button and wife (Lise had split for L.A. the week before, and Button, soon after, suddenly developed a client in the south—nobody knew what had happened); two day doormen; Rudy; Gramps, and a few other regulars; a reporter from the San Jose *Mercury* with a cameraman and a few dudes I didn't recognize, probably plainclothes men. All together there were close to fifty people, counting the dancers and Obie's crowd. It was a good houseful.

The wedding party showed up from the church around eleven-thirty, leading with the topaz and the nineteen chips. Everyone cheered, and champagne corks started popping the balloons. Gerry stood in back of Libby, with his hand over hers on a knife aimed at a big cake. Paula clicked a Polaroid. Obie went into the office and opened all the taps. The meters began to click.

Callie must have come without my noticing, because the first I saw of her was when she walked out of the dressing room carrying what looked like an antitank gun in its case. I'd known it was supposed to happen but it still took me a minute to believe my eyes.

Callie was wearing a long black thing that looked like the type of expensive relic fallen on hard times that chicks love to drag home from bargain shops. I had the feeling that for the first time I was seeing one bought new.

Pat followed her up on stage with her accordion, wearing white fur hot pants and a transparent shirt. Three other girls went up: Delise with a tambourine, Fat Mary with a gourd, and Toni with a kazoo.

Callie set up her chair in front of the outsize pillow kept back there for the girls who liked to hump a pillow as an occasional change of pace. She sat down and started tuning. "What are you doing?" Whitey yelled up. "Aren't you supposed to play them things standing up?"

The girls stared at each other. They didn't know what to do next.

"TAKE IT OFF!" voices yelled.

"Can you do soul on that thing?" Pat said.

Callie shook her head.

"Do you know 'Finiculi Finicula'?" Negative. " 'The Tennesse Waltz'? 'Old Man River'? 'Chop-Sticks'? Well fuck, I can't do none of that lah-de-dah opera stuff. Don't you know *nothing* popular?"

"Oh, dear, I'm sorry, no. . . . I beg your pardon. I do. I know one popular song for the cello," said Callie, raising her bow. And amidst the cheering and hoots and red lights winking reflections off the polished wood, she launched into "The Swan."

The deep cello voice sang out over Obie's, that broad cello vibrato, like fucking on a water bed.

A black swan raised its wings and took off ponderously from the cracked surface of the water.

It had to be a put-on, but I wasn't sure. Could anyone be pure enough to bring a real swan to Obie's?

The audience and the other musicians stood and gaped as Callie, oblivious, sawed away. Suddenly Pat raised her accordion.

Fantastic! Under the transparent blouse her hard little boobs were leaping like trout as she pushed and pulled. I think she was playing the theme from *Shaft*.

Toni hit the kazoo.

There were two different keys and four different rhythms going on up there, not counting the lights and Pat's boobs. The kazoo sounded like the sirens in "D.O.A.," the tambourine banged away with the grim regularity of the Salvation Army Band, the gourd had me right back in Acapulco with "Enchilada Lotta," and through it all the cello sawed serenely on. The whole thing reminded me of something that never failed to crack me up when I was very young, my mother playing "The Blue Danube Waltz" with her right hand and "Over the Waves" with her left.

"March, march!" yelled Whitey, doubled up. The girls looked at each other and started marching around Callie in her black recital gown, swaying in a small time warp to Carnegie Hall as they bopped and jived and jingled around her.

The music straggled to a stop. Everyone cheered and stomped and clapped. The girls were stunned by their own success.

"Don't say anything," gasped Callie as I handed her a beer. "At least that's the first time I ever played on a stage without fainting."

The formal entertainment over, they turned up the jukebox and started to wail. I don't know exactly how it got started, but suddenly couples were forming and going up on stage, one after another, while the rest sat below watching, yelling and clapping.

Delise and Benny went up and danced. Delise was wearing a mini-dress that clung to her ass with heartbreaking fidelity. Benny was wearing gray silk pants and a lacy shirt that showed skin through the patterns. Delise went into her usual piston-stroke number, but her hands were talking and that toothsome ass snapped from side to side in ecstasy. Matteo once said that the difference between playing by yourself and with another musician was like the difference between masturbating and fucking. That was the difference between the girls dancing by themselves and the way they were going at it now, with partners.

I was standing next to Callie, clapping and yelling together with everybody else, and then Whitey was strong-arming me toward the stairs. Laughing, sloshed, I let myself be pushed.

Once up there, though, I froze. I looked down at the upturned faces, red, glittering, mouths wet with beer and enjoyment. It seemed like they were nothing but heads, upturned heads, open mouths and staring eyes. I looked around, and there they were in back of me too, a funhouse crowd in the wavy mirror. I looked up and saw the lights: hot, blinding, winking.

My skin prickled. The vibes were incredible. I had a very clear picture of myself standing naked, shaking my dick at the crowd like one dancer who used to take a fold of flesh in her hand and jerk her boobs up and down manually.

I wanted to get down. But Callie was standing there, waiting to dance.

I'm no kind of dancer. I play a good game of tennis and I'm a good climber, but something happens to my coordination when I try to dance. I do this mother-pheasant-distracting-hunters shuffle with one leg dragging, a movement a chick once told me was a variation of something called the Bermuda Boogaloo.

Callie, that lovely mimic, picked up on it right away and we Bermuda Boogalooed away, two birds pretending to be lame. I liked the way she adjusted her movements to mine, and I started playing with her, bending backward so she'd have to lean over, then forward again, pressing her down. I pushed her so far she almost lost her balance. I put a hand on her back to steady her. I let it rest there, at the top of her ass, as we danced, feeling the dress and the skin and the muscles slide.

When the music ended I was caught by surprise. People cheered. I felt foolish, then good. I was blooded. I'd earned the right to sit down and give other couples a hard time.

Finally, amid cheers and howls, Libby and Gerry got up on stage. Libby looked beautiful and outrageously happy, and I felt a pang about letting that ass out of my bed unplowed. Sex *la vive*. Someone else had it now.

"H9!" Libby yelled happily, and on came my all-time candidate for all-around inanity and insult to the ear, although I had to admit appropriate for the first time in its ill-conceived existence—some chick singing with predatory cheerfulness:

> "I hear those churchbells ringing, ringing tenderly,
> Won't you carry me—won't you marry me tenderly . . ."

Libby did her thumper rabbit dance while Gerry spun on his heel and went into crouches, a sort of choreographed karate. His jacket flew open, and I thought I saw a handle sticking out of his waistband.

In the middle of the song there're a few bars of *Lohengrin,* then the music stops dead while the drummer whacks a lead-in, BAM BAM BAM BAM! Back to "carry me—marry me."

On the BAM BAM BAM BAM Libby abandoned a slightly bridal reserve and did four outrageous bumps, facing right toward the audience. And the guests also abandoned a certain nuptial respect and yelled as one:

"TAKE IT OFF!"

"Take it off" by now was getting generic, a sort of "right on," the Obie's *olé.* Nobody really wanted Libby to climb out of her panties at her own wedding reception. But that's what she did. A little drunk, very happy, she chugalugged a beer someone handed her up, yelled "G7!" and proceeded to divest herself of veil, dress, slip, and bra. When she was down to panties, long white plastic boots, and the cross on a chain around her neck, Gerry ripped his tie off and threw it into the audience.

"TAKE IT OFF!"

Libby unlaced her boots.

"TAKE IT OFF!"

Gerry pulled his belt out of his pants.

"TAKE IT OFF!"

By the time Libby was naked Gerry was down to his shorts and socks.

"TAKE IT *OFF* TAKE IT *OFF* TAKE IT *OFF* TAKE IT *OFF* ..."

The drunkest, happiest crowd Obie's had ever seen was in a frenzy. It was jungle fever, not the plastic recording-studio variety, but real fever, jungle fever, hot for consummation and oblivion, dagger and birth, the circle of skulls and the tongue dripping blood. Beer mugs banged, feet stamped, hands beat together, throats howled, a ring of savages in the jungle clearing, and in the middle two naked people dancing, man and woman, us joining in them.

This, finally, was what Obie's, even in its sad and crippled way, was all about.

But what the fuck, I remember thinking, pushing my way somewhere through bodies and bodies, so what if it's dirty and crummy and sad. Here I've been taken in, accepted, not because I have talent, no demands, no expectations, just me sitting at the door. My own mother walked out on me, but an ex-dancer makes me tea when I have a cold; my own brother left without looking back, but a semipimp took me in off the road.

I'm in the men's room refusing to feel sentimental while I'm hopscotching puddles of piss on the floor, but it's no use. I can't decide whether I'm in here to pee or cry.

Over the trough someone had pinned a card:

> **IN CASE OF AIR ATTACK HIDE UNDER THE URINAL —NO ONE'S HIT IT YET.**

Weeping, I pissed all over my shoes.

Then, or later, Button was standing next to me at the trough in his check suit.

"How's it going, Button?"

"You know I just got back from L.A., don't you. I saw Lise. That poor creature. She finally broke down and told me why our love couldn't be."

"Oh, no!"

"Those filthy Communists. Torturing an innocent girl like that. Do you know before they'd let her out of the country she was gang-banged by an entire regiment? That's just for starters. Some of the things they did to her she can't even talk about to this day. In case you ever wondered, that's why she can't make it with men. But didn't it look to you like she liked me, Pete? She said if it hadn't have been for what those bastards did to her . . ."

Champagne dripped out of his eyes and ran down his Winnie-the-Pooh cheeks.

It made me glad. Man, woman, or depilated gorilla, beneath the silicone knockers Lise had a heart after all.

Later I ran into Paula behind the bar, and we hugged, rocking, patting each other on the back, consoling each other for obscure reasons. With nothing intervening, I was sitting in one of the gravel dog runs behind the Sinema, staring at a wall that

191

said *Freedom Laundry and Dry Cleaner* and thinking about all the other dogs that sat there looking at that sign while they waited for someone to come and take them home.

In the ripeness of time, Gerry and Libby took off in the GTO, which subsequently took first prize in San Jose's decoration competition for Most Vulgar Wedding Vehicle of the Year.

Around five o'clock, anyone still upright started helping clean up. At six o'clock we opened up. Pretty soon the first lonely, horny dude ducked in the door.

A dancer got up on stage and started to dance.

I'd come across the article in a *Chronicle* left on a table at Leroy's:

STERN AT THE GROVE
Isaac Stern returns to his native city for a special free concert with the San Francisco Symphony at 2 p.m. next Sunday in Stern Grove (named for Sigmund, not Isaac). Stern will play Beethoven's Romance No. 1 and Bruch's Violin Concerto No. 1 under conductor Leon Fleisher, also a native San Franciscan. . . .

This had to be it, this Stern cubed, this cosmic confluence of Sterns, sun in Sigmund, moon in Isaac, and Peter rising.

I showed Callie the article and said I was going and she said it certainly looked exciting, and I said I'd keep an eye out for her by the gate then.

That Sunday—it was a week after the wedding—I was up early washing pants and a shirt at the laundromat down the block. After breakfast I scrubbed maniacally under the shower, shaved twice, debated about the cologne—behaved, in fact, just like that day seven years and at least that many cunts ago when I flew across the city on jets of deodorant to dedicate my cherry to Matteo's upcoming recital.

The whole time I was planning the seduction. Whitey had laid a few doobies on me for the occasion, and I had a fresh fifth of George Dickel No. 12 in my pocket. The only problem was where.

Never back to San Jose, never never Toomy's Transient Hotel. I assumed Berkeley was out, too. It was more than a year since I'd lived in the city, and even if my friends were where I'd left them, I couldn't dig showing up at the door a year later with a "Howdy, mind if I fuck in your living room?"

That left the great outdoors. I knew plenty of spots right in Golden Gate Park from the weekends in my teens when I biked feverishly mile after mile looking for a girl to save from something, anything, after which she'd fuck the shit out of me in gratitude. No, fucking in the park was for hippies. What do you do with a full-grown woman?

You take her to a motel. No. After Palm Oak Court, for me motels meant bunches of weirdos playing musical cubicles. A hotel, then. One of the ritzy ones. After the concert, my dear, drinks at the Top of the Mark. Leaning over, I lace her Shirley Temple with George Dickel. On the way down I stop the elevator at the floor where I've already reserved a room. Suavely, I . . . no.

I finally decided not to sweat it. If the feeling was right we'd make it in the back of the VW if we had to.

I hitched up to the city around twelve. My ride took the Broadway exit, and we drove into the city past all the skin joints, the famous strip where it all started. I'd been through here hundreds of times, but with the knowledge I had now I really *saw* the thing for the first time. As we inched along in the Sunday traffic my insides crawled.

One Obie's after another! Two-city-blocks-on-both-sides-worth of Obie's! Twenty, thirty Obie's in a row, but without the small-town oafishness which, despite a degree of crumminess that would never pass here, preserved in Obie's a certain crude innocence. These places were sophisticated in their pandering, out to titillate the real flesh-eaters, the big city weirdos, jungle cats to our San Jose toms.

The signs battled for attention in letters a foot high:

I hitched over to the other side of town. Here the houses were luxurious; there was space; there were trees, broad streets. I remembered coming here with my mother to watch puppet shows. I must have been very little.

I sat on the grass inside the entrance to the Grove and watched people arriving for the concert. I watched a kid walking with his parents. He probably studied the violin, too, the three of them cherishing the same lonely exaltation. The faces were out of my past, solid, comfortable men and women, with deep voices and lots of laugh lines. They reminded me of when we were still a family, Robert and I kicking each other between our parents at the Civic Auditorium, a concert at the Opera House.

I heard a violin somewhere near—Stern warming up behind a eucalyptus? I walked toward the sound, and there was a young guy with round glasses and a coat down to his ankles, with his music stand set up on the grass. A little crowd had gathered around him, and every once in a while someone put some money in the case he had open in front of him.

I stood for a while and listened. I smiled at a pretty girl with a violin case in her hand, an insider's smile. I'd done this Haydn myself, and I knew just where he'd run into trouble. Sure enough; he missed the difficult shift on the D string and had to go back over it. I put a dollar in the case and went back to look for Callie.

The people were really pouring in now. I'd probably miss her even if she came. Then I saw her while she was still walking on the street a block away. She was wearing something very short, and her legs were ten miles long. Men were looking at her, but her walk had no awareness of being watched. She hadn't grown up to what had been happening to her these past few months. She had no vanity, this lovely woman coming toward me with the uncertain smile.

"Peter! There must be thousands of people here. It's lucky we caught each other. How are you?"

"I've been looking forward to this very much."

"Me too. Isaac Stern! Can I ask a dumb question? Is he any relation?"

I fought with the mother inside me and shook my head.

We walked down the path to the Grove. It wasn't

really steep—old ladies were capering down ahead of us—but Callie grabbed my arm and dug her feet in. We threaded forward to the benches and sat down.

"Isn't this exciting," Callie said, and I agreed, taking advantage of how exciting it was to touch her, a hand on her arm to point out a lady in the cello section in a pink dress and big sunbonnet, leaning toward her to see something and keeping the contact.

Actually, a certain excitement did start inside me as I watched the orchestra tune up. I knew how it felt to be part of that tremendous concentration about to find completion. If duets was fucking, playing in an orchestra was a goddam orgy. And soloist with an orchestra—it's got to be like one man balling a hundred women simultaneously.

Stern Grove is a natural amphitheater at the bottom of layer upon layer of eucalyptus, and when the orchestra started playing the trees played along with it. The cellos swayed, the trees swayed. The violins plucked and the wind plucked, sending snows of seed fuzz down through the sunlight. Some kid in back was blowing bubbles, and the wind carried them slowly past us, one by one spinning past showers of seeds and spiraling into the trees.

Then Uncle Isaac himself came out, round as a bubble. The crowd welcomed him. He spoke about coming to San Francisco. Then he raised his violin.

It was as if I'd never heard a violin before.

How long since I had been to a concert, any concert? Even listened to a record? But it wasn't just that. I think maybe it was Obie's. I think maybe the long hours under the amplifier, my ears being pounded clean the way you pound clothes on a rock by the stream, reamed and steam-cleaned of thirteen years' worth of sophistication. I listened like a baby, with my innocent ears. It was like being on acid. I was holding Callie's hand, and I must have been squeezing like a maniac, but she hung in there.

When he stopped playing I knew one thing at least. I had a vocation. It wasn't just Mother taking her revenge on old In-and-Out by perverting his children with music. Not just an overdisciplined kid trying to pipe his mother back home. It might take me years just to get back to where I had been when I stopped playing, and even that was a gamble, but for better or worse I knew what my thing was.

Callie and I were standing up; people were standing all around us, clapping, clapping. We hugged each other, clapped some more. We moved with the crowd, being carried up and up, out of the grove, high in the park like a crowd of grass-blowing hippies after a rock concert. The crowd thinned, and we were back on our own momentum. I was beginning to think about how to introduce the topic of hotels when Callie said, "Peter, would you like to come on a little errand with me? My grandmother's away on her annual fifty-five-day cruise and there's no one looking after the house but the Filipino cook and my grandmother's sixty-year-old nephew, Kenny. They tend to stay drunk together the whole time she's gone and forget to do things like water the plants. Now that I'm in the city I should really look in."

I took her arm and we started walking. It was a perfect San Francisco day, the type you only read about in the paper when you lived in the perpetual fog of Pneumonia Gulch. I was high on revelation and anticipation. I had enough money to take us out later to a good dinner at my favorite place in North

Beach, an Italian restaurant with no menu, just big women who brought you food as soon as you sat down. It had been a long time since I'd been there. It had been a long time since I had walked through my city with a chick I wasn't just out to fuck.

Things probably started to go wrong in the car. Callie was a hundred times more horrendous on hills, stalling at the top of impossible inclines and sending long shudders through the line of cars behind as she slipped backward trying for first.

"Believe it or not, I'm really much better than the first time I drove in the city," she said brightly. "The first time I went down one of these hills I stopped every three feet and pulled into a driveway to pee in my pants."

"Would you like me to drive? I've been doing these hills since I was sixteen."

"No! I mean, no thank you. Goodness, why are all men like this? How will I ever learn anything?"

"All men," I took it, were me and her husband.

Grandma's house was another bummer. It was a narrow, three-story townhouse, fairly new, in a block of identical neighbors. They might have all been away on cruises. No one was around, not even cars, and late Sunday afternoon sat heavy as Pneumonia Gulch fog on the empty sidewalks.

The front door opened onto a dark hall filled with furniture, rugs, vases, all kinds of shit. There was a staircase leading to the main floor; from what I could see, it was also draped and cluttered.

"Uncle Kenny! Tio!" Callie called up the stairs. "They must be out getting drunk somewhere. Granny takes the key to the liquor cabinet with her."

She led me past the stairs to the back of the house. This must have been planned as a storage or utility area—one door opened onto the garage—but it was fixed up as a little apartment: a living room, a tiny kitchen with a cutout wall for serving. The room was a box with one high window, wall-board, linoleum on the floor, and three pieces of furniture: a couch and two chairs, Sears Roebuck Modern. It was surprising after the baroque hallway.

Callie went straight to the icebox, rummaging and talking over her shoulder.

"There's not much. Coke, ginger ale. Do you like artichoke hearts? Listen, if you're really hungry there's probably something upstairs. I just always prefer it down here. When my grandmother moved from the old house she wouldn't part with a stick of furniture, and that house was about three times bigger than this. This is the only room in the house you can walk two feet in a straight line without bumping into something."

I sat down in a striped chair, got back up again. There were framed photographs along one wall. I flashed on the poses.

To Samuel and Jenna Mandelbaum—
My sincere best wishes.
Nathan Milstein, N.Y.C., 1946

To Jenna Mandelbaum, in fond remembrance of a pleasant afternoon.
Yehudi Menuhin, January 1945

Zino Francescatti, Patricia Travers, even old Isaac, all posing with their violins. And this was the fucking basement. Who was hanging upstairs?

I was a postman's son from Pneumonia Gulch. Four years ago I'd given up my right to look those photographs in the eye. This was someone else's woman chatting nervously about artichoke hearts, and I was finding it harder than when I was seventeen.

Suddenly I felt very lonely. I needed something warm and sentient.

"Callie! Cut all this bullshit and come out here."

She came, clutching a box of Triskets like a shield.

I took the box out of her hands and put it on the floor and put my arms around her. There was no response. Her muscles were rigid.

I stood back. Callie was looking at the floor.

"Peter, we need to talk. I've never done this before. I'm sorry. I married the first man I ever slept with. In this day and age. There it is."

"No talk, Callie. Help me do this."

"Stop it, Peter. What are we doing taking my clothes off? You don't know me. You don't even know about my children. Let me tell you something totally irrelevant. When Sara was a tiny baby and she had a cold we used to put her between us and lie awake all night, so we could check if she was still breathing."

She was wringing her hands wretchedly.

"Would it help if I left a dollar at the door?"

Why did I say that? Was it supposed to be a joke? Or did I mean it? For four months I'd sat at the door handing out tickets. I might have been Circe handing out spells that turned men into animals. Because I sat there sneering at them in my heart didn't make me immune.

Callie shuddered like that time at the door and started to run. I grabbed her and pushed her down on a chair. I didn't want to rip the dress. It looked brand new. For this occasion? Never mind. She's a dancer, just a dancer.

She was wearing a bra. I shook her hands off and

pulled it down. I was sitting on her thighs. She was crying. It was like something you do in your father's car. Disgusted, I got up. She stayed slumped there, her head turned aside.

"Get out of here, Peter," she sobbed.

I started to walk away, then I turned back and looked at her. Poor big dumb cunt. I was sorry for both of us. We'd both blown it. Before I split I wanted to do something good for her. I wanted her to feel something. I wanted to beat Obie's.

I knelt down again. She was totally passive, head turned aside, hiding her eyes. I kissed her all over her face, her neck, down her breasts, to her nipples again. I stuck my hand down and felt her cunt. It was dry and tight as an asshole. I spit on my fingers and rubbed inside the slit, searching for the slippery little handle. I had to keep stopping to wet my fingers. When I got back down there it was all closed again.

We twisted onto the linoleum. I smelled its dusty, waxy smell, and I smelled the other, sour and yeasty, like San Francisco bread. I tried to sooth her, stroked her face. Finally she opened her eyes, brimming with tears.

Beat Obie's. Big joke. I *was* Obie's. Rolling around on the linoleum, the blood pounding in my ears, the smell of yeast and sweat, darkness in my mind. I was Obie's, mirrored in the cracked eyes of a dancer.

One morning, the summer I lived with Linda, I was wandering the streets trying to work off adrenalin from one of our fights when I came across a billboard in front of a church where they usually advertise the topic of Sunday's sermon. All this one had were the words:

HAVE YOU DONE WRONG? THEN DO RIGHT.

What simple and comforting advice for this merry-go-round of fuck-ups. The good cancels out the bad. We're not doomed forever by our small lacks of grace. A practical salvation. Have you done wrong? Then do right.

I went back home with a rose for Linda.

But I wasn't sure what I could do right for Callie. It would have been better for both of us if she'd fought, screamed, scratched my face, called the cops. Anything but the way she just lay there, resisting only passively, a dumb childbirth gripping of the thighs as I worked her over, like someone pumping on a swimmer who's been under too long.

It was the same passivity I'd watched one night when Obie grabbed her as she passed and started examining her points like a horse you're thinking of buying, and she stood patiently under his pawing like a newly broken horse, nervous but docile.

"Not bad, huh? Not bad!" he yelled. "I like 'em big myself for a change of pace. What's your name, baby? Curly! I like that. Only you ain't short and curly, you're tall and curly. Got you by the tall and curlies, Curly!" And he did, while she just stood there, and the crones looked on sipping their Cokes.

Hundreds of men had touched her against her will, with their hands and their wants; there was no way she could defend herself but turn numb to it. She had finally accepted that valuation of herself: she was meat. To herself she was meat. We were both "Obies" that Sunday afternoon, going through the only motions we could, each of us in our solitary dance.

Maybe that was the last straw. Maybe it was just the end of a long winter, five months of ten-hour nights, five nights a week, which had to be some kind of world's record in this profession. Callie lasted till spring, then the spirit drained out of her all at once.

She did the same dance, made the same movements. The guys saw cunt and tits, that's all. She was just one of the girls, the tall one, tired, mask-faced. She came raving to Slate one night, some guy had pinched her or something and she wanted him kicked out.

"You cool it," Slate said to Callie, flicking her breast with his fingers. "You not here to give the customers a hard time."

Another time a guy groped her, and she took a

swing at him with a beer mug. The guy ducked and laughed. It might have been a joke, but I saw the look in her eyes. He was lucky she missed.

She was out sick with a cold for three nights. When she came back she looked worn out. She seemed to have lost another twenty pounds all at once.

The cold went into her throat. She sounded like Miss R.H. long ago, and she danced with a scarf around her neck.

"TAKE IT *ALL* OFF!" yelled the usual nitwit, and so one time Callie unwrapped the scarf and threw it in the corner, and she took off her wedding ring and threw it down, and her shoes, and I thought maybe she'd recovered a little of her sense of humor, but then she reached down and pulled out a Tampax, and she yelled in that ghastly voice, "Now all I have left is my I.U.D., which I'd be glad to remove for your enjoyment, but since I can't, fuck you! Sincerely and from the bottom of my heart, *fuck fuck fuck fuck fuck every one of you!*" She was shaking, and the tears were running down her cheeks.

Like "D.O.A.," Callie had O.D.'d on Obie's.

In the normal course of things she would have had to cut down or stop for a while anyhow. Pulling crawling females off the walls was nothing new around here, but when a girl's bummer started bumming out the customers too, they got rid of her. Fate just hastened things along.

Callie had a little number where she bent over backward, facing the wall, until her head was over the edge of the stage, and then she stretched out, her arms reaching toward the audience. She used to have fun with it, waving at the dudes upside down, sticking a finger in somebody's beer. Now it was

205

mechanical, like most of her movements these days.

One night when things had been heavy all evening, a demon Monday, some drunk grabbed the outstretched hand. Callie tried to sit up, but she was off balance. She let out a shriek.

We came running from three ends of the bar: Joe from the office, Slate from the pool table, me from the door.

Callie was stretched at a downward angle, her feet still on the stage, her shoulders on the little bar. She fell into the thronging, excited front row just as Slate grabbed the nearest dude by the scruff.

"Hey, man!" he yelped. "I was just trying to help."

I'd seen how he'd been helping. I saw them all helping. She'd been wearing her whole costume when she went down. When we got to her she was naked; they'd ripped everything off her, including her shoes. Left alone, they would have raped her, one after the other, right there on the floor, in the slops and spilled ashtrays.

We got her to her feet. She was moaning and holding her ribs. Something had hit her in the side as she fell.

One of the girls helped her to the bathroom, where she pissed blood.

"Jesus, she shouldn't been reaching over like that in the first place!" said the manager. "It's against the six-feet rule. We're lucky we didn't get busted."

Up on stage, the next dancer was taking off her top.

Callie got dressed and split so fast she was gone before I turned around. She even left her bank in the drawer, with her tips in it.

Callie didn't show up the next night, or the next, or the next.

"She don't let us know pretty soon, she's off the schedule," said the manager.

"Give me her number," I said. "I'll call her up and see what gives."

"If I had her number I'd call myself. Look and see—they got Libby's number down for both of them."

I waited a week. On the blackboard in the office the line marked Callie disappeared.

I called Berkely information and asked for Zipser. An answering service told me to state my business with the doctor at the sound of the tone.

I called Libby at the motel. She used to have the number but it was lost somewhere. She forgot the exact address but she could describe where the house was. I wrote it down.

I waited a few more days, then I hitched up to Berkeley. I got rides as far as Cedar Street and started into the hills on foot. It was Sunday. Berkeley was sunny and quiet. People dressed in a way I hadn't seen for months—ladies in long pastel dresses, men in dark suits, little boys with crew cuts—stood around outside a church. The men were smiling, and the pastel ladies chatted.

Men were out working on their lawns. I asked directions a couple of times. Through a window I saw a woman in a robe with a coffee pot in her hand.

A basset with a jingling chain joined me for a few blocks. I climbed higher, and the houses grew more elegant. They stood close together behind wide lawns. There were little white flowers in the grass. Cars hid in shadowy garages.

Callie's house was on a corner, just as Libby had said, a big stone house with gables and peaks and green shutters, like something out of a German fairy tale. Trees hugged the stone, and there was green all around it, shrubs and lawn and ferns. It was a cool, established-looking house, quiet behind the green windows.

The mailbox said J. D. Zipser, M.D. I started up the path, already talking in my head—your tips, just happened to be passing, we wondered how you were. But who passed this high? What did the D stand for?

I pictured the man I had seen that night, wearing a robe and pajamas, bunching his lip and beard in that compulsive way while I waited my chance to corner his wife alone, when can I see you, *psssss psssss!*

I stopped walking. It was so quiet I heard my heart pinging inside me like a pot just out of the kiln cracking in the cold. I was alone, as always, on the outside looking in, and my heart was breaking, and I was happy.

Mother had been answering me all along. She split without me because, like Greta Garbo sprinkling grass seeds on her head with wild abandon, she vanted to be a-lawn. If it was a sickness, like Paula said, then it was hereditary.

I turned and walked back down the hill.

That night I told Whitey I'd be moving on in a week or two. This time he asked me if there wasn't any chance I would stay. They could use all the hands they had because next month Globe A-Go-Go was opening at ten o'clock in the morning.

"Ten o'clock! You're joking."

"Don't count on it. You wait and see, they'll be lining up outside at nine-thirty. All the businessmen bring their out-of-state clients around, they go, 'Hey, bet you guys don't see nothing like this back East.'

Stick around, Pete. Obie's been talking about you. I've got all I can handle with the movies and the agency. How would you dig being General Manager?"

Obie's got his eye on you. . . . To be one of the boys, like Gerry, like Whitey, adopted into the business, taken in, that paternal pat on the cheek. Jesus, it was tempting. But it was time to do without fathers, too.

Libby got the word from Berkeley that Callie was all right—she'd had X-rays taken, her kidney had been bruised, nothing that wouldn't clear up. But she wasn't planning on coming back to work. Whitey was pissed because of the band, but then some chick stumbled in off the street for a dancing job who turned out to play a mean autoharp.

For a while one or two guys a night asked where the tall one was. Then the waves closed over.

I don't know yet where I'll be heading, but whether it's fiddling on a street corner or a salmon boat, I plan to be back to look Callie up when I figure she's had enough time to get her shit together. I'm sure she'll make it down to the coast somewhere—she's a stronger lady than she knows, my Calliope—and as I sit here under the flashing lights I like to think of her in a little house with her children by the sea, where the surf goes boom boom boom and the wild rabbits run lickety-split through the marshes and away.